RAISING THE HORSEMAN

By SERENA VALENTINO

LOS ANGELES   NEW YORK

First Edition, September 2022
10 9 8 7 6 5 4 3 2 1
FAC-004510-22203

Printed in the United States of America

This book in set in Garamond LT 3 Pro/Linotype
Designed by Phil Buchanan

Library of Congress Cataloging-in-Publication Control Number: 2022933556
ISBN 978-1-368-05461-4

Reinforced binding

Visit www.DisneyBooks.com

Dedicated to my beloved Justin Sane. May our love endure beyond the grave as we haunt the imaginations of those who read our stories, long after we are gone from this world.

PROLOGUE
SLEEPY HOLLOW

I f the fine denizens of Sleepy Hollow are to be
believed, every single person who lives here has had
at least one supernatural experience. It's a ghostly
place still firmly rooted in its past, steeped in tradition
and superstition. It's a dreamlike and drowsy town only
disturbed by the ghosts and shadows that still haunt it.
Something holds sway over the people who live there; it
fills their minds with dark stories, strange visions, and
bizarre beliefs. The town of Sleepy Hollow, many say,
is haunted.

There are some haunted by memories, some by
tradition, while others insist they are haunted by the
spirits of this ghostly place. Some tell tales of having
witnessed the apparitions of dead soldiers replaying
their last moments on the battlefield, or a sinister set

of eyes peering at them from the hollow of an old tree, or of hearing whispers dancing on the breeze just over their shoulders while they walk deserted forest paths. But the spirit that seems to dominate their minds and imaginations most is the phantom of a headless man astride a black spectral horse. The Headless Horseman.

It's believed he was a Hessian trooper who lost his head to cannon fire during the Revolutionary War. It's a ghastly image: the poor man's head being carried away by a cannonball, never to be found again. This spirit haunts the nightmares of the children of Sleepy Hollow, only to creep back into their dreamscapes years later when they are adults.

The Hessian's body was buried in the churchyard, and it is rumored his ghost travels from his resting place to the scene of the battle in search of his head. But by all accounts, this ghost isn't confined to reliving his final moments or restricted to wandering the same paths again and again: The Headless Horseman has been seen astride his dark steed on forest paths and dark roads, both common and rarely used, and often on the almost entirely hidden path that leads to the Oldest Tree, one of Sleepy Hollow's most cherished landmarks.

For beneath that tree, half-hidden behind the twisted

low-hanging branches, many residents of Sleepy Hollow say they have seen the ghost of Katrina Van Tassel whispering to the spirit of the Headless Horseman, who some believe resides within the venerable oak.

ONE

THE LONGEST TWILIGHT

Make no mistake about it—this isn't Ichabod Crane's story. Oh, sure, he blunders in and out of our tale, tripping over the pages and making the usual fool of himself, but this adventure belongs to Katrina Van Tassel and her granddaughter many times over, Kat Van Tassel.

Kat's tale begins when she is eighteen, on the two hundredth anniversary of Katrina Van Tassel's death—the night known in Sleepy Hollow as the Longest Twilight. Like many in the little town of Sleepy Hollow, Katrina loved twilight, the time between day and night right before you are expected to be snug in your home, safe from the apparitions that creep out of the shadows when the darkness comes.

According to the legend, on the night Katrina died,

the last vestiges of twilight stretched on until midnight, the Witching Hour: a time when the dead come out of their hiding places and move among us, a time when anything is possible. Not since Katrina's death has twilight stretched so far, but the people of Sleepy Hollow still call the anniversary of her death the Longest Twilight.

Kat Van Tassel grew up with these traditions and superstitions. She had heard stories about Katrina and the ghosts of Sleepy Hollow since she was a little girl. As far back as she could remember, the town would gather together to decorate Katrina's grave with her favorite flowers on the Longest Twilight. When Kat was five, she had asked her mother why everyone in town took sprigs of those flowers home with them to hang above their doorways. *To appease the Headless Horseman,* her mother said. *The legend says the ghost will pass your house by as long as you pay proper tribute to his dearest love, Katrina.*

Five-year-old Kat had closed her eyes tight, and tried not to think about what would happen if he *didn't* pass their house, a thought that would haunt her until she no longer believed in ghosts.

The Longest Twilight was one of the most revered traditions in Sleepy Hollow, second only to the Van Tassel

Annual Harvest Ball, which always followed a few days after. And on the night Kat's story begins, the Van Tassels had been preparing for the ball in a fevered frenzy, pausing for the evening to pay their respects to their ancestor Katrina Van Tassel. The Longest Twilight was not a night for harvesting pumpkins to carve, planning menus, sewing costumes, and hiring bands. It was a night to dim the lights and sit by the fire, an evening of stories, and of peering out windows in hopes of catching a glimpse of the Headless Horseman. It was a night the eldest members of the family told stories about the great Katrina Van Tassel.

However, the festivities did not go on as Kat's parents would have liked, for everyone had been at the cemetery to honor Katrina except Kat. Right before twilight ended, Kat came bounding into the house in her usual fashion, causing a great commotion by dropping her pile of books with a loud thump before thundering up the stairs to her bedroom.

"Kat Van Tassel, don't you dare go off to your room. You come down here this instant!" Kat's mother, Trina, always got this way when preparing for the Harvest Ball, and Kat had been hoping to avoid her this evening. She was late, and she knew it. "Great Hollow's Ghost,

Kat, you are testing my patience; now get down here!" her mother bellowed from the kitchen.

"Yes, Mom?" Kat asked as she peered into the room a moment later.

"Home right before dark, as usual," said her mother, putting down a stack of papers she had just been looking at.

"I lost track of time reading."

Kat's mother opened the oven and looked in.

"What's for dinner tonight?" Kat added, trying to distract her mom from the tirade she knew was coming to her after arriving home so late and missing the Longest Twilight celebration at the cemetery.

"You know very well what's for dinner! We have it every year on this night! Katrina's favorite, chicken with olives and garlic. Speaking of which, where were you when we decorated Katrina's tomb earlier? Everyone kept asking, 'Where's Kat? Where's Katrina's namesake?'"

Kat sighed. "We're all Katrina's namesake, Mom."

Kat's mother closed the oven, took off her apron, and put her hands on her hips. "That's right. And you're a bit too much like her if you ask me!"

Kat felt bad that she hadn't met her family in the

cemetery to decorate Katrina's grave, as they did every year in the late afternoon on the Longest Twilight. In her mother's opinion, that tradition was the most important part of the Longest Twilight celebration, and Kat missed it. She hadn't intended to; time had just slipped away while she was reading, and now she felt bad.

"I'm sorry, Mom, I really should have been there. Is there anything I can do to help?"

Her mother smiled. "You can put the sprigs of flowers over the doorway outside. They're on the dining room table."

Kat went into the dining room, where the table was already set. The light was still golden outside, making the room look warm, like it was already glowing with candlelight. She saw the flowers sitting there, bound together by a purple ribbon. She loved the scent of them, thick and heavenly and filling the room.

As she was walking toward the front door, her father, Artis, burst in like a bear in stocking feet, which made Kat laugh because that is what his name meant—*bear*. "Kat! It's almost dark; get those flowers up immediately! And where's your mother? I have to talk with her about something!"

Kat laughed at her father. He was such a strong,

sturdy man, and gruff most of the time, but she couldn't take him seriously in his stocking feet. Kat's mother demanded long ago that he take off his boots before coming into the house if he had been out in the fields with his workers. Which of course he didn't need to do, but insisted upon it anyway. *The Van Tassels are working people,* he would say. Even if they did have more money than anyone else in the county, her mother and father tried to live their life modestly.

"She's in the kitchen. *Where she always is.*" Kat said the latter half under her breath. She went outside and hung the flowers on the black wrought-iron hook that had been there since she could remember. For all she knew, it had been there when the original Katrina was a little girl.

Kat stood there looking at the flowers, wondering if the Headless Horseman was real. She wondered what would become of her life, living on her family's estate like all the other Katrinas before her.

All the women in the family were named after the first Katrina Van Tassel, and they had all found ways to make their names more individual. Kat's mother, for example, went by Trina, and Kat's grandmother was Kate. The original Katrina had decided in her time that the succession of inheritance would go to the firstborn daughter of every generation, but they couldn't inherit unless they were named after her and they kept the name Van Tassel. Which would mean the men who married into the family would have to be pretty open-minded, especially during the generations when such a thing was unheard of, but then again, it took a special kind of person to marry a *Katrina*.

Kat hated having her fate already decided for her. If previous generations of Van Tassel women were any guide, she would spend the rest of her life on this estate, and marry a man who would oversee the farm, numerous crops, and enterprises. If she had an interest in farming and the running of an estate, then she didn't see why she couldn't just run things herself! But the fact was, she wanted to go away to school—her family, though, insisted she stay in Sleepy Hollow and receive her education at Ichabod Crane High from teachers who taught her nothing of the world because they had never ventured outside of Sleepy Hollow.

Kat thought it was ridiculous that her high school was named after the most historically hated man in Sleepy Hollow. But the name was a warning about what may befall those who didn't take the Legend of

Sleepy Hollow seriously. Crane High offered the usual array of subjects found at any other high school, however there was always some sort of supernatural aspect that seemed to eclipse the subject at hand. Math, for example, included the study of numerology and divination through the use of numbers. The history curriculum always highlighted historical legends both in and outside of Sleepy Hollow (including from places with high supernatural activity like New Orleans and San Francisco). Why ghost stories were considered "historical events" was beyond Kat's comprehension. Kat didn't believe in ghosts, but her teachers and classmates didn't share her skepticism, or if they did, they didn't make it known. And since it was the only school in Sleepy Hollow, she had to attend the high school founded by Ichabod Crane.

Despite being a nonbeliever, Kat loved a good story, no matter its subject, and she made it her business to read as much as she could. She would slip away as often as possible, sit at her favorite café or by the Oldest Tree, and read. She read all manner of books, fairy tales, mysteries, ghost stories (just because she didn't believe them didn't mean she didn't enjoy them), science fiction, romance, vampire stories, anything she could get her hands on. And that's what they were to her: stories. Fiction. Just like the stories she grew up with in Sleepy Hollow. But her true passion was nonfiction. She loved reading about other countries, their monarchs, and history. Not their legends, but the actual events that took place. And she had a large collection of travel books. She loved sitting for hours just reading about all the places she would love to visit but feared she would never see.

Life felt small to Kat, every day doing the same things, seeing the same people, walking the same paths, and as much as she loved it, sitting under the same tree, and hearing the same ghost stories on the same nights every year. Books were a way to make her life feel larger. A way to escape.

"Kat! What are you doing just standing there, daydreaming as usual? Light the candles and shut out the lights. You act as if we've never celebrated the Longest Twilight," her father grumbled as he came back into the dining room. Kat sighed and went to the fireplace, taking a long matchstick from its box. She struck it along the side and watched the flame burst to life. She went about the room lighting all the candles and then turned off the lights. Every year, she remembered how much she loved this room by candlelight, the way the flames cast shadows on the walls. Sometimes she could swear she saw Katrina's silhouette in the shadows. She remembered being a little girl and watching the candle-light dancing on the walls while she listened to her family tell the Longest Twilight story, and she was sure they were surrounded by ghosts. And then it occurred to her that everyone in Sleepy Hollow was doing the same thing she and her family were this evening, sitting in candlelit rooms, watching the flames and shadows dance, and telling stories about Katrina Van Tassel the First. She longed for the days when she still believed in all the old stories, and wondered exactly when she had started to doubt they were real.

"Kat, go help your mother bring dinner to the table." Kat's father was a hulking man with rough hands and a weatherworn face from all the time he spent outdoors. But Kat thought he was a handsome man even if the lines in his face resembled chiseled rock, and his large, intense eyes always looked a little too serious. He was the perfect partner for her mother. Content to spend his life with the running of the farm while she dedi-cated her life to the running of the house. It was all a bit antiquated for Kat, but it seemed to work for her parents. They were quite the pair, the two of them, her father with his dark hair and eyes, often with a full dark beard, and his massive build and height, and her mother so small, soft, and round, all golden, and peaches and cream. Kat had inherited her father's height, dark eyes and hair, and his darker complexion. She was the first Katrina Van Tassel not to have blond hair, and she rather liked it.

Kat did as her father asked and went to the kitchen to help her mother. They could have a cook and a legion of servants if they wanted, but Kat's mother preferred to do almost everything herself. Of course, she would hire help for the Harvest Ball and other grand events, but the daily running of the house was entirely on her mother's shoulders, with one exception: Maddie, who had been with the Van Tassels for as long as Kat could remember. She was more her mother's companion than anything else, but she did help with the running of the house, making trips to the market, and helping Kat's mother with anything she might need. Maddie was an older woman, originally a part of Grandma Kate's household when the house was bursting with servants. Kat's mom couldn't bring herself to let the woman go because she had been more like a second mother to her than anything else, and she didn't want to deprive the woman of her wage, which she depended on since being widowed—and Kat's mom knew Maddie wouldn't accept money without working for it. Kat was happy to always have Maddie in the house—she loved her; really, she was like a grandmother to her. An opinionated, sassy grandmother, but a grandmother nevertheless.

"Where's Maddie, Mom?"

Kat's mother gave her a queer look. "I gave her the evening off to spend with her gentleman caller, of course. I fear we might lose Maddie to him. I can't imagine life without her," she said, brushing away a long strand of golden hair that had fallen into her face.

"'Gentleman caller'? Who even says that anymore?" Kat's mom made her laugh sometimes. The way she talked, it was as if they were still living in Katrina's day and not two hundred years later.

"Kat, stop teasing me. Can you please just take all these serving dishes to the table while I freshen up? I hate for your father to see me looking so untidy." Kat smiled at her mother. She thought her mother was beautiful. She looked like all the Katrinas before her: blond and buxom, with peachy skin and rosy cheeks. She wondered what the first Katrina would think of Kat's dark hair and long, willowy frame. She was so different from all the other Katrinas.

Kat took the serving dishes into the dining room, where her father was waiting. Kat loved this room, with its dark woodwork, built-in china hutch with china dating back to Katrina's time, and the grand, ornately carved dining table that was far too big for just the three of them. This house was built for entertaining, which they did quite often, but this evening it would just be family. Her father was standing at the fireplace and lighting his pipe. Ever since Kat was young she loved the smell of her father's pipe smoke, and she enjoyed watching it curl in billowing plumes, swirling and then filling the dining room. Her mother hated it and wished he would smoke his pipe outside. Family legend dictated there was a long line of men who smoked at the fireplace and wives who disapproved, which made Kat laugh because it seemed to her nothing in her family—or in Sleepy Hollow for that matter— ever changed. This was vividly and painfully illustrated every time her parents nudged her toward marriage, and she was gearing up for them to raise the topic again this evening. She was only eighteen, about to graduate from high school, and the last thing on her mind was getting married. But things ran differently in Sleepy Hollow, especially if you were a Van Tassel. Sometimes it felt to Kat that the world moved on without her, and indeed moved on without Sleepy Hollow, where time felt as if it had stopped.

"Your mother is off sprucing herself up, I suppose?" her father said, laughing.

"Yes, but you're not supposed to know that. You're to think she magically looks perfectly put together and beautiful even though she's been cooking all day."

Kat's father smiled. "Your mother always looks beautiful, sprucing or no." It made Kat happy her parents were so in love and seemed so content in their roles. "Where's Blake?" Her father looked at his watch. "It's not like him to be late."

Blake was Kat's boyfriend. Kat could hardly remember a time when Blake wasn't in her life. Every memory of her childhood included him, so it seemed natural that as they grew up, they would fall in love. He was like most of the young men in Sleepy Hollow: obsessed with the occult and the supernatural. He ran around with the Sleepy Hollow Boys trying to raise spirits from the dead, doing séances, and trying to find the resting place of the Headless Horseman's head. Of course, nothing ever came of it, but it seemed they had a good time winding each other up, playing elaborate pranks, and trying to make each other believe they had found the Hessian soldier's head.

Kat wondered if the Sleepy Hollow Boys thought that name was original, but who was she to comment on the unoriginality of names? She was, after all, one of many Katrina Van Tassels.

"I told him I would rather spend the evening alone with you and Mom tonight," Kat said as her mother came into the room.

"Blake isn't coming over this evening? Well, that's a shame." Kat's mother stood under the archway that separated the dining room from the library. She had refreshed her makeup and hair and looked perfect, as always.

"We don't have to spend every day together, Mom." Kat was annoyed. She knew what was coming.

"I suppose there will be time enough for that once you are married," her mother said, winking at Kat as she sat down at her place at the table.

"Who says I'm getting married, to Blake or anyone?"

Kat's father dropped his fork onto his plate with a clatter, causing her mother to jump.

"Now, now, don't upset your father. I'd hate for my china to pay the price for your insolence."

Kat took a deep breath. She didn't want to have this conversation again. "I'm not being rude, Mom. I'm just saying how I feel. I don't know if I ever want to get married. What's the big deal?"

Kat's father cleared his throat with a deep grumble. This was usually a cue that he was about to say something he felt was important and he wanted everyone's attention. "It's a very big deal, Kat. You have a legacy to uphold, traditions to pass down, and responsibility to this community. You and your future husband will have a duty to run this estate together after your mother and I step down. We employ most of the young men in this county, and a good number of the women depend on our crops to make their preserves and the baked goods that they sell to the city folk who visit here."

Kat rolled her eyes. "Do you even hear yourself, Dad? Men working in the fields, the women at home baking?" Both of her parents looked dumbfounded at her question.

"This is how it's been here for generations, my girl. I don't see what you're balking at. I'm getting old, Kat, I can't keep doing this forever. We need a younger man running things here so your mother and I can enjoy our twilight years, hopefully with little grandbabies bouncing on our knees."

The thought of having children, at least anytime in the near future, made Kat cringe. She loved her parents but hated how old-fashioned they were.

Kat got up from her seat, walked over to the window, and opened the curtains with a violent snap. All the curtains had been closed to protect against the spirit of the Hessian rider, and her parents gasped.

"The last thing I'm thinking about right now is marriage and having children. And honestly, I'm sick to death of talking about it, let alone all our traditions and superstitions. Have either of you seen the Headless Horseman even once? Do you actually believe the stories you tell on the Longest Twilight or on All Hallows' Eve? Tell me. Does anyone in this town? It's like some mass hallucination."

"Katrina! Close those curtains this instant!" Her mother ran over and shut the drapes herself.

"My name is Kat! And I'm not going to marry Blake

or anyone else just because you think I should." Kat stomped off and up the stairs to her room.

Her mother sighed heavily. "I'm sorry, darling. I'll go upstairs and talk to her." She kissed her husband on the cheek.

"Please talk some sense into her, Trina. I don't like what I see in that girl lately."

"Don't worry about Kat. She has a lot of the first Katrina in her." She put her hand tenderly on her husband's.

But Artis only frowned. "I know, my dear, and that's what worries me most."

⤳

Kat slammed her bedroom door behind her. She instantly felt silly for making such a fuss. It was typical teenage behavior, and Kat hated to be typical.

"Kat, can I come in?"

It was Kat's mom on the other side of her bedroom door. The last thing Kat wanted to do was talk to her mom, but she knew if she didn't let her in it would hurt her feelings and only make the situation worse.

"Come in."

Trina opened the door slowly, careful not to knock

over the many stacks of books by the door. Kat's room was filled with books, stacks of them everywhere, on her desk, on the floor, and in her window seat.

"Kat, you have too many books. You should really put these away in the library. It's getting crowded up here," her mom said, looking around the room and then sitting on the chair near the window. "What's gotten into you, Kat? Did you and Blake get into a fight? I don't understand where all of this is coming from. Saying you never want to marry? He's exactly the sort of man you should be happy to settle down with."

Kat got up from the bed, knocking over a pile of books and swearing under her breath.

"But that's just it, Mom. I don't think I ever want to get married. Especially not with you, Dad, and Blake pressuring me."

Kat's mother's eyes grew wide with excitement. "Has he asked you to marry him? Why didn't you tell me?"

Kat scoffed. "He hasn't asked, Mom. He just assumes we'll get married after we graduate, and honestly that's part of the problem. Everyone just assumes. I've never traveled outside of Sleepy Hollow, not once. Not even to go to the city. You and Dad won't let me. You believe we live in a haunted town, Mom, *a haunted town*; how dangerous would it be for me to visit New York City? Everyone here thinks we have a ghost who chops off people's heads, but you're afraid to let me go to college. It doesn't make sense."

"Kat, you're the heir to a great legacy. You have a duty not only to your family but to the people of this town. To the Legend of Sleepy Hollow itself!"

"Mom, you're acting like I'm an heir to the throne or something and it's my royal *duty*. Do you have any idea what century this is? You should be encouraging me to go to college, not pressuring me into getting married. I know people here get married after high school, but I don't want to be stuck here forever."

Kat's mother got up and went to the foot of the bed, where there was a large trunk. Kat had never opened it—she was supposed to wait until she was married—but her mother opened it now.

"What are you doing? We never open that," Kat said.

Her mother was busy looking for something and didn't answer.

"Here," she said finally, and pulled out a book. "Kat, I want you to read this."

"You just said I have too many books."

"This is the first Katrina's diary. You missed her ceremony this evening and pretty much made a debacle of dinner; the least you can do is read about the great woman you were named after, and once you're done reading her story, I want you to come to me and tell me if you think our traditions and stories are—what did you call it? A mass hallucination."

Kat smiled at her mom. Kat had been rotten at dinner and her mom was actually being pretty cool about it. She was right; it was the least Kat could do, even though she still planned to live her life as she chose. She didn't bother pointing out to her mother that if she did have a mind to stay in Sleepy Hollow and run things, wouldn't she be in a better position to do so with a college education? But there was no arguing with her parents on this topic, and she didn't want to keep her mom's hopes up about her sticking around. She was leaving one way or another.

"Thanks, Mom. I will read it." She put the book on the bed and stood up. "Sorry about dinner. Should we go downstairs? Dad is all alone down there waiting for us."

"You stay here and read Katrina's diary. I'll bring something up for you to eat in a little bit. Let's give you and your dad some time to cool off." Trina gave her a playful wink before she left. Kat's mom liked to wink; it was her thing, and Kat thought it was cute. There were a lot of things about her mom she liked, actually. She started to feel bad that she ruined the Longest Twilight, even if she felt she had a reason to be annoyed and angry with her parents.

Kat sighed and looked down at the book on the bed. It was a thick brown leather-bound book. Across the front, in gold lettering, it read: KATRINA VAN TASSEL. The gold lettering had started to flake away in spots, making it seem as though it read KAT VAN TASSEL, which made Kat smile, because Katrina was sitting in Kat's favorite spot, under the Oldest Tree, in the first diary entry Kat read.

TWO

THE DIARY OF KATRINA VAN TASSEL

SLEEPY HOLLOW GROVE

As I sit under the Oldest Tree, I can't help but be distracted by the beauty of the light and shadows dancing on the pages of my diary. My mind is elsewhere—back at home with my mother, reeling from what she said before I headed out the door to take my daily walk in the Sleepy Hollow Woods.

⌣

"Now, Katrina, do you really need so many books? A man never wants his wife to be smarter than him."

Katrina loathed when her mother said things like that. She was standing at the doorway, holding a great pile of books, aching to leave the house, wanting nothing

26

more than this conversation to be over with. It seemed almost daily Katrina's mother would bring up the topic of marriage, and she had done so again that morning. Not to mention how much Katrina hated the idea that women must pretend to be unintelligent for the sake of the men around them. Like somehow her love of reading made her unappealing. None of it made sense. Wouldn't it be better to have an intelligent, well-read partner, someone of substance, and with something of value to bring to their conversations? The notion that a woman's province was restricted to the keeping of her home, husband, and children was ludicrous to Katrina, and nothing she said made her mother understand her feelings on the topic.

"Who says I am going to marry anyone, Mama? And it's not my fault Brom can be a fool sometimes." Katrina's arms were piled high with books, and she was eager to get out the door. All she wanted was for her mother to stop pestering her so she could go read in peace.

"Oh, Katrina! Don't say such things. Abraham Van Brunt is a fine young man." Katrina always found it amusing when her mother used Brom's full name. Her mother was right, of course; he was a fine young man, by Sleepy Hollow standards at any rate, and certainly by her parents' standards. He was a bit of a town hero actually, though Katrina didn't understand why. Sure, he had won all sorts of sporting events, was an excellent hunter, hauled in more crops than any of the other young men who worked for her father, and was good at telling a ghost story, a talent most people in Sleepy Hollow tried to perfect. But a *hero*? That, she felt, was a bit of an exaggeration.

Since she was young, her parents and Brom's had been pushing the two of them together, but she was starting to doubt she loved him in the same way she had when they were younger. They used to spend their days under the Oldest Tree reading stories together and talking about the characters in their favorite books. They would explore old cemeteries and laugh at the names on the headstones. They would take long walks down Sleepy Hollow Road dangerously close to twilight, in hopes that they might catch a glimpse of the Headless Horseman. They talked of going off to college in New York, and of seeing the world. But as Brom got older, he lost his fondness for books and his adventurous spirit. Now he focused more on his job working for her father on the farm, and running around with those Sleepy

Hollow Boys. He seemed perfectly content to live their entire lives in the same little town, just like everyone else in Sleepy Hollow.

Now, as she sat under the Oldest Tree, she was at last at peace. She loved the oak grove, its trees towering and large, reaching out to each other like lovers. This was her sacred place, where she came to think, and read, and be herself. And as much as she loved Sleepy Hollow Grove, she loved the Oldest Tree even more, with its twisted and moss-covered branches that made her feel protected and safe. It seemed to Katrina the tree knew all her secrets, all her fears, and all her happiest moments, for she wrote about all of them while sitting under this tree.

She couldn't help but think about the conversation she had just had with her mother, and it made her miss the person Brom used to be and realize the reason she was so angry with her mother that morning. She felt she was trapped in a life that wasn't her own anymore, fated to marry a man she feared she was starting to despise. Everyone took it for granted she and Brom would marry. It was a matter of fact that no one bothered to consult her on. She often wondered if she would find herself jumping the broomstick with Brom, wondering how she had come to find herself married to him. She felt as if she was caught in a current that was taking her further and further from herself, each wave pulling her further away from her dreams.

She would sometimes daydream, wondering if things would be different between her and Brom once they were married, what he might be like with her in their own home, alone, and not under the influence of their parents or the Sleepy Hollow Boys. Perhaps then he would be more like the sweet boy she fell in love with, because there were times when she saw the man she once loved within him like strikes of lightning, making her heart happy, but today would not be one of those days.

She saw Brom standing on Sleepy Hollow Road as if she had summoned him simply by conjuring his image in her mind.

"Katrina!"

Speak of the devil. She closed her eyes tightly, trying to will him away, but alas she didn't possess the power to do so. Katrina opened her eyes, shielding them from the sunlight. He had clearly been out the whole night and was just now making his way back home with his group of friends.

"Hello, Brom," she said unenthusiastically, hoping he would just keep walking. She didn't like how he acted when he was around his friends, especially when he had been out all night rabble-rousing and drinking. "Aren't you going to come over and give me a kiss?" he called out to her. Behind him on the road, his friends were roughhousing. She tried to act as if she didn't hear him, but he came closer, while his friends jeered and whistled, teasing him because Katrina clearly wasn't interested in his advances. "Come on, Katrina, just one little kiss?" he asked, trying to be sweet and playful.

"Not now, Brom." Katrina sighed. "You know my dad would murder you if he caught us kissing."

He kept walking toward her, even though everything about her body language and tone of voice radiated that she wanted to be alone.

"Soon we won't have to worry about your father, Katrina, not after we're married," he said, kicking at the dirt on the path, causing it to stir and get all over her books.

"Brom! Look what you did!" Katrina was no longer pretending she wasn't annoyed, and Brom noticed.

"You and your precious books!" he said, and made a big show of laughing and looking back at his friends still roughhousing in the road. "What are you reading then? One of your romance stories? Let me see it." He grabbed for the book in her hand, which happened to be her diary.

"It's none of your business, Brom!" She pulled it away quickly, surprising him with how roughly she snatched it from his hands.

"I suppose you should get in as much reading as you can before we are married," said Brom.

"And what exactly do you mean by that?" She had told herself earlier if one more person had brought up the topic of marriage she would scream. But she didn't scream, she just felt numb and exhausted. She wished he would realize she had no desire to have this conversation, and just leave and rejoin his stupid friends.

"Well, it's not like you'll have much time for it," he said loudly, making a show for his friends, who started in with their yelps and whistles again. "You'll be too busy raising our children and taking care of the house."

The minute he said that, it was clear he knew he'd gone too far because Kat said nothing to him at first. Instead, she directed her rage at his friends. She was incensed.

"That's enough tomfoolery out of you!" Katrina

snapped at the Sleepy Hollow Boys. "And as for you, Abraham Van Brunt, who says I'm marrying you—or anyone?"

"Come on, Katrina, don't be like that. We're just having a bit of fun. Why do you always have to be so serious?" Brom looked down at his feet, kicking at the rocks in the road like a scolded child. Katrina could tell he felt bad for upsetting her—even if it was clear he didn't fully grasp why what he said was so offensive. But she knew he would never admit it in front of his friends.

They continued to tease him, calling out his name over and over. "Abraham! Oh, Abraham!" No one called him that but their mothers and Katrina, and only when she was angry at him.

"Why did you do that, Katrina? Now they're going to tease me all day."

It served him right. Katrina straightened the pile of books in her arms and gave him a hard look, searching for some hint of the boy she once loved so dearly. But alas there was no strike of lightning. Nothing about this conversation made her heart happy.

"Just go, Brom," she said, trying not to cry. "Just leave!"

"Do you want me to walk you home? It's getting

close to twilight." Katrina could see Brom was feeling bad, and she could always tell when he was trying to make things up to her without using words. He would offer to walk her home, carry her books for her, or simply take her by the hand and give her a sweet smile. This usually warmed her heart to him no matter what a fool he had been, but not this day. Today she wanted to hear the words. She wanted to hear he was sorry.

"No, Brom. I would like to walk alone."

THREE

THE BROKEN PROMISE

Kat put down Katrina's diary when she heard her mother come into the room. She looked around her room trying to root herself back in the present. Everything was as it should be, her carved oak desk, turntable, silent-movie posters, and walls lined with bookshelves stuffed with books and vinyl. She had been spending so much time in the past with Katrina she almost felt as if she were there, which made her room feel slightly unfamiliar to her at first. Kat's mom had prepared a plate and brought it in for Kat on a wooden tray. "You're reading Katrina's diary, then?" she asked, finding a spot on Kat's cluttered desk.

"Yeah, it's really interesting actually. I mean, we all know the Legend of Sleepy Hollow, the one we tell on All Hallows' Eve: how Ichabod Crane came rolling into town, threatening Brom's relationship with Katrina by wooing her, so Brom dressed up like the Headless Horseman to scare Ichabod away. But I've never thought of it from Katrina's point of view. We never talk about how Brom made her so unhappy."

Katrina's mother raised her eyebrow. "What makes you think Brom was dressed as the Headless Horseman? That's not part of the legend."

"Well, it wasn't an actual Headless Horseman, Mom." Kat grinned. "He doesn't exist. Ghosts aren't real."

"I wouldn't be so sure about that, Kat." Her mother went to the window, opening the curtain just a sliver and peeking out.

"Mom, do you really believe in him? The Headless Horseman, I mean."

Her mother closed the curtain and turned around. "You know I do, Kat. Promise me you will read all of Katrina's diary, and no matter how you feel once you're done reading, you will do as I say and always come home before dark." Kat had never seen her mother so serious.

"Don't I always, Mom?"

"Yes, you do, my sweet girl. Now eat your dinner;

it's getting cold. I'll be back to get your dishes later."
She turned to leave.

"Mom, is Dad really upset with me?"

"Don't worry about your dad, Kat. He's smarter
than you give him credit for. He understands. Of course,
you could have saved your outburst until after dinner
on the most important night of the year, but he'll get
over it. We both love you, Kat." She smiled as she closed
Kat's bedroom door. That's how her mother was. Always
smiling. Always making people feel better. It was no
wonder she was so loved in Sleepy Hollow. It had nothing to do with being the most prominent person in the
town. Sure, that probably helped, but she was a truly
good person and cared about the people in her community. She was a *true Katrina*. As with most people who
seemed happy all the time, Kat sometimes wondered
if it was all just an act, but her mom appeared to truly
love her life and Sleepy Hollow's traditions, which she
expertly preserved and cherished. She embraced her role
as a Katrina, and she did it well.

Kat sighed. She was different from the other
Katrinas. She knew that. She even reveled in it. But
there was still a part of her that wondered if she would
ever live up to their legacy, because there was a part of

her that wanted to carry it on. She just had to figure out how she could do that and live the life she wanted.

Kat was jarred out of her musings when she heard her phone ding. It was Blake's text tone. She hadn't looked at her phone once since she came home, and she forgot she was supposed to meet him at the cemetery for the ceremony, and later again that night, so when she took her phone out of her bag, she saw there were multiple texts from him.

Blake
3:31
Kat! Where are you?
3:33
Babe?!
3:35
I'm here, where are you? Your parents are SO MAD!
3:45
Kat!? WHERE ARE YOU?!

Kat
9:15
I'm so sorry! I lost track of time reading at the Oldest Tree

Blake
9:16
Seriously, Kat!?

Kat

9:17

I'm sorry

Blake

9:17

It was your stupid great-x-a million
grandma's thing and you didn't even show
up! What's wrong with you lately?

Kat

9:18

What's wrong with YOU? Why did you
even go if you think Katrina is stupid?

Blake

9:18

Stop overreacting, I'm so sick of it. Everyone is

Kat

9:19

Who exactly is *everyone*?

Blake

9:20

EVERYONE, KAT! EVERYONE thinks you're a
DRAMA QUEEN, you're always getting mad at
me for no reason! They all think you treat me
like crap! You're really selfish sometimes

Kat

9:27

I'm sorry. Please don't be mad at me.
I really did just lose track of time

Blake
9:28
So are you meeting us at the cemetery tonight
or are you going to flake on that, too?

Kat closed her eyes and sighed. She had told Blake they would go to the cemetery later, but she wasn't feeling up to it. She wanted to just stay home and read Katrina's diary. It felt like everyone was mad at her: Blake, all his friends, her dad, and even though she was being cool, she was pretty sure her mom was still upset with her, too. She really messed up not going to the Longest Twilight celebration at the cemetery with her family. She felt guilty about backing out on plans with Blake, but all she wanted was some time to herself. Maybe he was right and she was being selfish, but she just promised her mom she would stay in and read Katrina's diary.

Kat
9:32
I promised my mom I would stay home tonight.
She's really upset I missed the Longest Twilight

Blake
9:33
I knew you were going to flake

> **Kat**
> *9:34*
> I LITERALLY just promised my mom
> I wouldn't stay out after dark. She is
> afraid of the Headless Horseman

Blake
9:35
Whatever, you're a Katrina

> **Kat**
> *9:35*
> What you do mean?

Blake
9:37
You never pay attention in class, do you? The
Headless Horseman was in love with the first
Katrina, and promised to keep all the Katrinas after
her safe. That's why you're all named Katrina
9:38
Your mom needs to chill

Kat didn't remember learning that in class, but Blake was probably right; she usually zoned out when they talked about her family. It was bad enough being a Katrina in Sleepy Hollow, but it was even worse being a Katrina at Ichabod Crane High. It was like she was some sort of oddity, celebrity, or both. She honestly didn't know which. Blake loved it, of course, all the attention he got for being with the next "reigning Katrina," but all the attention made Kat uncomfortable, so she was happy that most of the time it was focused on Blake. The last thing she wanted to do was go to the cemetery on the Longest Twilight, with all of Blake's friends asking her questions about her family and making fools of themselves trying to coax the Headless Horseman out of hiding, giving them the wildest ghost story in modern Sleepy Hollow's history. Probably the only wild story they would ever have. And she wondered if they really believed in him anyway. If they did manage to summon him, wouldn't he just chop off their heads? Isn't that what the Horseman does? You'd think if they really believed he existed they would be afraid of him. But she didn't bother bringing that point up to Blake—he would just say she wasn't making sense, and maybe she wasn't. She didn't want him to be angry with her anymore, so she decided to go even though she didn't want to.

Kat
9:40
Fine. Want to meet me on my back porch
so we can walk over together?

Blake
9:42
Let's meet at the cemetery. I have some stuff to do

Kat
9:43
What stuff? I don't want to walk alone

Blake
9:44
Stuff, Kat. Why don't you ever trust me?

Kat
9:45
What are you talking about? I just
don't want to walk alone

Blake
9:45
Whatever, you don't even believe
in the Headless Horseman

Kat threw her phone down on the bed before she texted him something she would regret. She did trust Blake, but when he did stuff like this, it made her wonder if she should.

FOUR

WAKE THE DEAD

When Kat got to Sleepy Hollow Cemetery, the party was already well underway. She was struck by how beautiful the cemetery was, still decorated for the Longest Twilight: scattered among the tombstones were small hollowed-out pumpkins with candles glowing within, but the most remarkable spectacle was the first Katrina's grave site in the Van Tassel family mausoleum. It was surrounded by hundreds of glowing candles and adorned with flower wreaths made with love and admiration by the people of Sleepy Hollow. The scent of honeysuckle, jasmine, and lavender was intoxicating. The air was thick and almost sticky with the scent, and it made Kat's head swim.

Kat stood at the cemetery gates taking everything in before she entered, wanting to live in that moment for as long as she could, dazzled by the flickering flames of the candles like dancing ghosts. She was happy she was here to see this and felt bad she hadn't been there earlier to celebrate the Longest Twilight. Even though she didn't believe in ghosts or an afterlife, she found herself apologizing to the first Katrina, wishing she had been there to honor her earlier that evening. She felt she was starting to get to know her, and for the first time, the original Katrina felt like a real person and not just a legend.

As she slowly made her way closer to where Blake and his friends were gathered, the peace and beauty of the cemetery were diminishing. She hated seeing it filled with Blake's friends partying, with their music blaring, and their screams echoing into the darkness so loudly they could wake the dead. That was one of the reasons she doubted if they truly believed in the legends, because if they did, wouldn't they fear the wrath of the Headless Horseman? As she stood there, she wondered what the first Katrina would think. The red plastic cups balancing on headstones, the mess they had already made, all of it felt so disrespectful. She hated everything about it, and now she hated that she was there. And she had a feeling Katrina would hate it, too. And just then she thought she saw something: a glimpse of someone, maybe a woman, standing in the clearing of the oak grove, looking at her. She had such a sad look on her face, it made Kat want to cry. She felt a chill run through her body, making her shiver and pull the collar of her coat up around her neck.

"It's beautiful here, isn't it? I mean, aside from all the rubbish," said a voice from behind her, making her spin around. She had thought for a moment the woman from the clearing was now behind her, but of course that was impossible. "Oh, I'm so sorry, I didn't mean to frighten you." said a young woman with long, straight black hair and large catlike eyes. "I'm Isadora Crow." Kat couldn't help but notice Isadora's deep crescent-shaped dimples when she smiled, one on each cheek. She felt silly because she had thought, just for the briefest of moments, that Isadora was the woman she had seen in the oak grove. Even Kat, who didn't believe in ghosts, sometimes let the atmosphere in Sleepy Hollow get to her. She looked to the clearing in the grove, but she didn't see anyone there and wondered who the woman could've been.

"Did you see someone standing over there, near the oak trees?" asked Kat, still feeling a bit spooked.

"I didn't see anyone. Perhaps it was one of Sleepy Hollow's ghosts," said the mysterious raven-haired girl.

"I'm sorry," Kat said, feeling silly now for being so spooked. "Hi, I'm Kat Van Tassel." To her surprise, Isadora flinched at the mention of her name.

"Oh! I heard you would be here, but I didn't expect—"

Kat knew what she was going to say even though Isadora cut herself off. "You expected a buxom blond, right?" Kat laughed, trying to make light of it.

"Well, yeah," said Isadora, making Kat laugh harder.

"Yeah, all the Katrinas before me were curvy blond little goddesses. I'm the first lanky brunette." She wondered why she was even having this conversation with someone she hardly knew. She had seen Isadora around school, but they hadn't met yet.

"Well, I think you're perfect as you are," said Isadora with a smile that sent a spark almost like lightning through Kat's entire body. Isadora said she was *perfect*, which made Kat giddy, not knowing exactly why or what else to say. She had been trying to find a way to introduce herself to Isadora since she arrived at school, but people got so weird about her being a Katrina, she gave up on the idea of making real friends, and sort of settled for Blake's even though she didn't really care for them. Isadora continued, pulling Kat out of her thoughts. "My family and I just moved here recently. I overheard at the celebration earlier there was going to be a party here tonight, so I thought I'd crash." She looked a little sheepish.

"Well, you're not crashing if you're my guest. My boyfriend and his friends are throwing this party. Let's join them."

Isadora gave Kat a funny look. "Right, but this is a party for your grandmother, isn't it? So, it's like *your* party."

Kat laughed. "Not really. This is Blake's thing. I'd rather be home reading right now."

Isadora smiled. "I think we have a lot in common, Kat Van Tassel."

Kat narrowed her eyes.

"If you'd rather be home reading then what are you doing here?" Isadora asked playfully.

"I could ask the same of you."

Kat had an impulse to grab Isadora by the hand to lead her over to the family crypt, where everyone was gathered, but decided against it. She'd just met this girl but she had already decided she wanted to be her friend.

"I didn't see you today at the Longest Twilight," said Isadora as she and Kat made their way over to Blake and his friends. The music and their voices were getting louder and disrupting the peace and beauty of the cemetery, at least for Kat. She didn't like hanging out with large groups of people. At least not this group of people. It always made her exhausted being in large groups, and she never knew what to talk about. She didn't have much in common with Blake's friends, and that's what they were: Blake's friends. Half the time she just felt like she was along for the ride, but it was a ride she didn't enjoy.

"Yeah, I'm a horrible Katrina. I missed my own great-great-great-great-great-great-grandmother's celebration," she said, laughing.

"I'm not sure that was the right amount of greats," said Isadora.

"Yeah, around my house we just call her *the first Katrina*. If my mom gets really sentimental she calls her Grammy. I probably wouldn't have come tonight, but Blake really wanted me to. Why aren't you home reading?"

"Honestly, I was hoping I would meet someone. It's hard making friends in Sleepy Hollow."

Kat knew how she felt, and hoped they would become friends.

As they got closer to Katrina's crypt, she could see there was a line of salt around it, which made Kat roll her eyes. Blake and his friends were standing in a semi-circle around the crypt, right outside of the salt circle, holding candles in their hands and chanting something she couldn't quite make out.

"Are they trying to summon the first Katrina?" Isadora looked as if she wanted to turn around and leave, like she was scared. Kat was just annoyed. She hated when the Sleepy Hollow Boys did this sort of thing, making fools of themselves with their chants and incantations, always trying to involve her. They had it in their heads she was the key to summoning the spirits of Sleepy Hollow, and they were always trying to make her take part in their stupid rituals.

"I don't know," she answered, shaking her head. But she did know that was exactly what they were trying to do. Even if Blake didn't think so, she did pay attention in class, and she knew a summoning circle when she saw one.

"Do you think that's a good idea? They have salt around her crypt so her spirit can't escape. What do you think they're up to?" said Isadora, taking a strand of her long hair and twirling it in her fingers nervously. Kat didn't understand why she was so anxious.

"Do you actually believe in this kind of stuff?" asked Kat. She had hoped since Isadora wasn't from Sleepy Hollow, she wouldn't fall for all this supernatural nonsense. But Isadora looked surprised at the question.

"Yeah, don't you? You grew up here, right? You have to have seen ghosts."

"I've never seen a ghost. Not one," said Kat, wondering if that was true. When she was younger, she was sure she had seen plenty of ghosts, just like everyone else in Sleepy Hollow, but as she got older, she wondered if she wasn't just succumbing to some sort of hallucinatory affliction brought on by living in a town obsessed by the occult.

"You don't sound so sure," said Isadora.

"I think it would be sad to be a ghost, don't you? The idea of becoming a ghost and being stuck here even after I'm dead gives me so much anxiety." Kat felt her heart start to race just thinking about it.

"Who says you'd be trapped here?" said Isadora with a worried look on her face. She was really starting to look panicked, and Kat wondered if they shouldn't just leave.

"Hey, are you okay?" Kat asked, but before Isadora could answer, Blake interrupted them, calling out to them from the crypt.

"Kat! Get over here. We've been waiting for you! We need your help. We're about to summon the first Katrina."

"I thought you said you didn't know what they were doing?" asked Isadora, twisting her hair between her fingers so fast it was hard for Kat to focus on what she was saying.

"I didn't know they were planning this." Kat felt uncomfortable once they reached Blake and the others. They always made her feel like she didn't belong, but this evening it was even more tense, probably because she had Isadora with her. The Sleepy Hollow Boys didn't like outsiders.

"Oh, look what the Kat dragged in; it's Isadora Crow!" said Blake, laughing. "What's the matter, Crow, afraid of ghosts?" Blake's friends joined in the laughter. Kat hated the Sleepy Hollow Boys' obsession with the occult. It didn't feel genuine, like it was some kind of joke, or a way to be popular. And she was pretty sure the only reason they tolerated her was because she was *a Katrina*, otherwise none of them would have probably given her a second look. They'd much rather be partying in a cemetery than reading in one.

"Blake, can I talk to you, over there?" Kat didn't want to talk in front of the others.

"Yeah, what's up? Everyone is waiting," he said, looking at his friends. All of them were whispering, probably wondering why she brought Isadora.

"Maybe she doesn't want to talk in front of everyone," said Isadora. Kat didn't know Isadora well, but she struck her as someone who had a hard time keeping what she felt to herself.

"Oh yeah, Crow, you think you know my girlfriend better than I do?" Blake's sharp tone made Kat flinch.

Kat noticed Blake was becoming more like his friends, acting like a jerk, and making fun of people who weren't like them. He wasn't always like that, at least she didn't think he was. He certainly wasn't like that when they were young. Now it seemed like he had disdain for anyone who wasn't like him, who didn't dress or act like him and his friends, and most especially for anyone who wasn't from Sleepy Hollow. Isadora Crow was an outsider, and that made Blake distrust her. People in Sleepy Hollow could be that way. Their only experiences with people outside of Sleepy Hollow were tourists, or distant relations who lived in other places, but they were basically tourists, too. Even Kat felt they were treated like an oddity, something of a spectacle, like they were all expected to put on a spooky show for them. It was just something they had to endure, since Sleepy Hollow relied so heavily on tourism. But she didn't think it was an excuse to be such a jerk to Isadora. She lived here now, and she seemed pretty awesome to Kat.

"What the hell, Blake? What's your problem?" He didn't say anything, he just narrowed his eyes at Isadora.

"It's fine, Kat," Isadora said. "Don't worry about it." Isadora looked as if she was afraid to leave Kat alone with Blake.

"Can we talk alone?" Blake took Kat by the arm in an attempt to lead her out of earshot of Isadora, who didn't take her eyes off them, and it made Kat uncomfortable because she feared Isadora could still hear them. She hated arguing with Blake in front of other people.

"What are you doing here with *her*?" he said through clenched teeth. "Everyone knows she's a *freak*!"

"I don't! What's your problem, Blake? Why are acting like this?"

"I'm pissed because you flaked on me and made me look stupid waiting for you twice today. You promised you'd be here in time to help summon the first Katrina, but instead you've been hanging out with Crow?"

Kat didn't remember saying she would help Blake
and his friends with their ridiculous summoning. He
knew it was the last thing she would want to do. But
now she wondered if she *had* promised and forgotten.
Why else would he be so angry?

"We've been waiting since ten, so we started without you. But I don't think it works unless a Katrina is
present for the summoning," he said, trying to lead her
back over to his friends.

"I don't remember saying I would do this, Blake."
She felt embarrassed having this conversation in front
of Isadora and the others, so she tried to make her voice
small so at least his friends didn't hear. They already
thought she treated Blake like crap, and it felt like stuff
like this always happened in front of them. "You know
I don't like this kind of thing."

"Oh, is Princess Katrina too scared to help us with
our ceremony?" yelled one of Blake's friends, causing
the others join in.

"Yeah, is a *Katrina* afraid of ghosts?"

"Why don't you shut up!" Isadora's cat eyes flashed.

"Why don't you stay out of this, Crow!" Blake
lashed back.

"Blake, this is crazy," Kat said, trying to stay calm. "You know I would never do something like this; why did you tell them I would?"

Blake looked at her as if she was losing her mind. "How do you not remember? We talked about this, Kat. I told you I wanted to try to summon the first Katrina after dinner. You totally agreed and said you'd be here at ten; you must have forgotten, like you forgot to meet me here earlier for the Longest Twilight celebration." Kat felt her stomach drop. It was a sickening feeling she felt whenever Blake reminded her of something she had completely forgotten. It felt like she had been forgetting a lot of things lately.

"I don't remember having that conversation with you," she said, glancing at Isadora and then back at Blake, keenly aware how she must be looking to Isadora.

"Kat, you know you're always forgetting things. Besides you're the most important part of the incantation. We can't do it without a *Katrina,*" said Blake, softening his tone.

"It's true. I am always forgetting things." She didn't know why she said that. Was she trying to protect Blake, or herself? She knew she would never agree to do this, but she couldn't argue she wasn't forgetful, because she was.

"Well, *I* don't think this ceremony is a good idea," Isadora said, fidgeting with the strap of her purse. "It seems disrespectful, waking Katrina from her rest on the anniversary of her death. Won't the Headless Horseman be angry? And what's with the salt around her crypt? Do you think she's stupid enough to let herself be trapped by a bunch of teenagers? What do you have planned anyway?"

"You're not as dumb as you look, Crow! We just wanted to ask her a few questions," he said.

His friends became rowdier, demanding Kat join them. "Kat, Kat, Kat, Kat!" They were all chanting her name, and it was making Kat's head spin. She couldn't think. She was already feeling nervous about forgetting Blake asked her to do this, and now with his friends being jerks she couldn't think at all.

"I think Isadora might be right; maybe this isn't a good idea." Kat's heart was pounding and she wanted to cry. She hated forgetting things, and she hated hurting Blake's feelings even more, but she didn't want to do this ceremony with them. Even if she had promised, even if she really forgot, something about it felt wrong to her. She didn't know what to do. She didn't want to make a scene in front of everyone, but she also didn't want to let them pressure her into something she didn't want to do.

"I'm going to look like an ass if you don't help us after I promised you would. I promised them *a Katrina*."

Kat sighed.

"Fine. Go tell your friends I'll be there in a moment," she said, feeling so angry with herself it made her want to cry.

"Please don't cry, Kat. You know I hate it. It's so manipulative."

Isadora gave Blake a seething look, and Kat thought for sure she was going to punch him in the face for saying that.

"I'm fine," Kat said, looking at Isadora, then at Blake. "Just go, I'll be there in a moment." Kat watched Blake walk away and willed the tears not to fall. She always felt a surge of panic when she forgot something she had promised to do for him. It made her feel dizzy and unable to think, like her mind was being hijacked.

When they were alone, Isadora turned to Kat. "He's the one manipulating you, you realize that, right?"

"You don't know him," said Kat, trying to clear her head.

"I know his type," said Isadora. "Please don't let them pressure you into doing this." She reached her hand out to take Kat's, looking over at Blake and the others to see if they were looking at them. "Don't doubt yourself, Kat. You shouldn't have to do anything you don't want just to make other people happy." Kat thought that was ironic because she felt that was exactly what she had been doing her entire life. It was as if others' happiness was entirely in her hands. It was always a matter of a choice between her happiness and someone else's, and she wondered when she would start choosing herself.

"It's not like I'm actually going to summon her," Kat said. "None of this stuff is real. It's all just games to them; I don't think they actually believe or else they'd be afraid of the Headless Horseman like you said." Isadora scoffed and glared in Blake's direction. "Will you stay with me?" Kat asked her, not entirely sure why she had aside from an inexplicable feeling Isadora was her only real friend there, even though they had just met.

But of course, Isadora wasn't her only friend. She was feeling irrational and anxious, which usually caused Kat to have thoughts she couldn't control, telling her something was wrong, even when everything was fine. She would feel better later; she would realize she and Blake were fine; she knew this was her fault, she just needed to mentally talk herself down. Right now, she just needed someone she felt comfortable with.

"Sure, I'll stay. As long as you're sure you want to do this." Isadora was looking around like she was truly afraid. Kat didn't want to make her stay if she was that uncomfortable.

"Are you scared?"

Isadora stood there for a moment not saying anything, her eyes shifting from Kat to Blake and his friends. "I am afraid," she said.

"You don't have to stay if you don't want to, but I promise nothing will happen. I'll say some words and literally *nothing will happen*. Ghosts don't exist."

Kat stood with the others, holding her candle in front of the Van Tassel family mausoleum, where all the Katrinas before her had been interred. It was unlike the other aboveground crypts in the cemetery. It was fashioned to look like the Van Tassel home but not quite to scale, which always made Kat feel uneasy. She saw her name across the doorway in bold letters: VAN TASSEL, and it made her feel slightly queasy. The sky was a deep purple with black clouds, and the moon was shining brightly above, casting an eerie glow on the white marble statue of Katrina that stood before the crypt, giving it the illusion of life. It suddenly occurred to Kat that one day she would be put to rest there, too, and wondered if future Katrinas would stand there remembering her, or worse, trying to summon her spirit. She felt a panic surge though her—maybe she had it all wrong and ghosts were real. But she quickly banished the thought because it was the usual nonsense that flooded her mind when she was nervous. She looked around fearfully, feeling as if someone was watching her, wondering if it was the woman she saw in the oak grove. She was feeling nervous and her mind was racing, going places she knew weren't logical.

"Kat, what's wrong with you? Say the words." Blake nudged her with his shoulder. She was standing directly in front of the door of the crypt, with Isadora and Blake on either side of her.

Something about being right in front of the crypt door was unnerving, and she felt her hands trembling. She wasn't afraid she was going to raise the first

Katrina's spirit, but she was afraid of not living her life fully before she was sequestered away with all the other Katrinas, trapped forever in Sleepy Hollow. She felt as if she was living her own nightmare, facing what she dreaded most. Facing the door that led to eternity.

"Are you okay, Kat?" Isadora reached over and put her hand on her arm and squeezed it. "You don't have to do this."

"Shut up, Crow! Of course she's okay," said Blake. "Say the words, Kat."

Kat's heart was thumping so hard she thought she would pass out. The door was moving in and out of focus, and for a moment, she felt as if she was back at home, just as afraid of being trapped there as she was in the mausoleum. Even the oak trees she so dearly loved looked menacing in that moment, their branches like sinister hands waiting to snatch her and toss her into a grave. But she swallowed her fear and said the words anyway, her voice cracking.

"Katrina Van Tassel, the first of our name, come forth from beyond the veil and show yourself to us."

Kat felt faint; the pounding in her chest was relentless, and it was sending fear though her entire body as the sound became louder and louder. But then she realized it wasn't just her heart she was hearing: It was the sound of a horse galloping their way, its hooves unmistakably pounding into the ground. She wasn't the only one who heard the strange noise; everyone panicked, some of them dropping their candles, which extinguished as they hit the ground. Others scattered into the wood, their candles bobbing through the branches like tiny points of light. Kat and Isadora were the only ones left in the circle; they stood alone now in the dark, clutching hands in fear. They were frozen as they watched an image materialize out of the candlelit woods: an enormous black horse galloping toward them.

"It's the Headless Horseman!" Isadora tried to pull Kat out of the way, but Kat was mesmerized by the concurrent sounds of her heart and the galloping horse. She just stood there staring at it, watching it rush toward her, until it suddenly stopped short about ten feet from where Kat and Isadora were standing. She could see the horse's hot breath coming from its nostrils, and its eyes shone red in the candlelight, making it look otherworldly. It reared up, smashing its hooves hard on the path as a gust of wind swept through the cemetery, causing the dried leaves to stir and the candles to extinguish. It was now almost pitch-dark except for a sliver of moonlight peeking from behind a bloodred cloud. They couldn't see if the horse had a rider, though it seemed to Kat there might have been someone astride this dark horse, and it sent a familiar chill to her core.

"Who's there?" Kat asked, trying to see into the darkness. She could swear there was someone on the horse, but it was too dark to see. "Is someone there?"

"It's the Headless Horseman!" Isadora's eyes grew wild with fear. "He's here to take revenge!" Kat could feel Isadora's hand tremble in hers, and she wanted to say something to comfort her, but she couldn't take her eyes off the horse. Its eyes were blazing in the darkness, and it seemed to Kat the horse was trying to tell her something. She didn't know how she knew this; it was something she just felt, as the chill in her body made her teeth chatter and her muscles seize.

"We have to hide, Kat! Now!" Isadora pulled Kat away from the horse toward the entrance of Katrina's crypt, her feet sliding on the salt that lined the ground, but Kat wouldn't go in. She'd rather take her chances with the demon horse.

"I'm not going in there!" she said, standing her ground. Ever since Kat was young, something about that doorway frightened her. She'd rather face the

Headless Horseman himself than go into that crypt. She felt foolish for feeling that way, like something of her past self still lived within her, where all the legends, superstitions, and family stories were hidden, in a secret place in her heart she was too afraid to access. "I don't think he's going to hurt us," Kat whispered, still shaking from the cold that seemed to penetrate her entire being. "He probably just got loose and wants someone to bring him back home." She didn't even hear Isadora's desperate pleas for them to leave, she was so transfixed. "You're not going to hurt us, are you?" said Kat, slowly making her way to the horse, reaching out her hand as the horse grunted hot breath into the chilly air.

"Kat, stop it! Come back!" Isadora sounded terrified. She could hear her voice coming up behind her. "Kat, please! It's the Headless Horseman. *He's going to kill us,*" she whispered, now at her side.

Kat reached out her hand and moved slowly toward the horse, her hand shaking as she tried to make out if there was someone astride it. Just as she thought she could see someone, the horse reared up, slamming its hooves hard on the dirt before it dashed away down the cemetery path and into the woods. In the darkness, she could barely make out the figure of a woman on the horse, her hair blowing in the wind behind her. *Who is that?* She wanted to go after the mysterious woman, but Isadora was slumped to the ground crying, weeping so hard she was coughing and trying to catch her breath. Kat sat down beside her and took her into her arms.

"I'm so sorry." She hugged Isadora tightly until she stopped crying. "Everything is okay. It's gone now." She hadn't realized how truly terrified Isadora was.

Eventually, Isadora's sobbing subsided. Kat felt horrible for how upset she was and beat herself up for asking Isadora to stay even though she had admitted she was scared. "I'm so sorry, Isadora. Are you okay? Do you want me to walk you home?" She looked into Isadora's beautiful eyes and noticed how sad they were, how frightened. She went to take her hand, but Isadora snatched it away quickly.

"You're reckless, Kat Van Tassel! You could have gotten us both killed!" Isadora was shaking with anger.

"I'm sorry you were so scared, Isadora, but the horse wasn't going to hurt us." Kat wiped away the last of her tears and pushed her long black hair out of her face. She looked exhausted and frustrated.

"Kat, I know you don't believe in the Horseman, or ghosts, or any of it, but you and your friends are messing around with dangerous magic, and it's foolish, especially if you don't know what you're doing."

Kat felt a surge of anger strike her like an electric shock. She was tired of people talking to her like she was an idiot. She was tired of always being told what to do.

"To hell with you!" she said, walking away from Isadora, then turning around to rail on her again. "How dare you call me foolish? I'm so sick of hearing that! You don't even know me." Kat stormed off toward the cemetery gates.

"Kat, wait, I'm sorry. I didn't mean to say *you* were foolish." Kat could see Isadora was being honest even if she was still angry. She waited at the cemetery gates for Isadora to catch up to her.

"Speaking of fools, where are Blake and all the other brave ghost hunters?" Kat laughed.

"Right? He just ran off with the others, screaming like little kids in a spook house."

"Come on, Isadora Crow, I don't blame you for being angry with me, but please let me walk you home. It's the least I can do after frightening you half to death," said Kat, smiling at her.

⌣

After getting back from walking Isadora home from the cemetery, Kat looked at her phone to see a text from Isadora asking Kat if she got home okay. There were no texts from Blake. She didn't feel like talking to either of them. All she wanted to do was get back to reading Katrina's diary.

She snuck back into the house without her parents hearing, got into pj's, snuggled into bed, and found where she had left off in Katrina's story. But before she started reading, she sent Blake and Isadora the same text:

Home now. Good night.

Kat felt a pang in her stomach when she thought of Isadora, and she wondered if she should ask how she was doing. She hoped she was okay. The girls hadn't talked much on their walk. It was awkward and uncomfortable. Kat was sure Isadora was still mad at her, and Kat was just mad, about everything. She was angry with her parents for hounding her about her responsibilities to the estate, angry with Blake for being a jerk, and angry because she saw her relationship through Isadora's eyes, and she didn't like what she saw. And she was embarrassed Isadora thought she was foolish, even if she said she didn't mean it. What else could she possibly think of her after staying with someone for so long who treated her like that? So, she'd said nothing, or next to nothing, as they walked. Isadora was still pretty spooked after everything that happened; she was jumping at every little noise as they made their way down Sleepy Hollow Road. The last thing Isadora needed was to listen to Kat talk nervously, when she probably had no intention of wanting to be friends, not after everything that happened.

"This is where the Headless Horseman attacked Ichabod Crane, isn't it?" Isadora asked, looking around as if she was expecting to see him coming down the path any moment.

"Everyone knows it was really Brom who scared Crane off. The Horseman isn't real," Kat said, giving Isadora the side-eye, trying to determine if she was warming up to Kat again.

"That's one theory. I thought most people in Sleepy Hollow thought it was the Headless Horseman, though," said Isadora.

Kat rolled her eyes. She was still feeling angry and wanted to have at least one conversation that didn't involve the Headless Horseman this evening.

"Do you think Katrina really liked Crane, or was

she just trying to make Brom jealous, like the legend implies?" asked Isadora.

"I always assumed she liked him, but I honestly don't understand why." As Kat heard herself, she knew her tone was curt, but she couldn't stop herself. She was filled with so much anger. She didn't know who she was more upset with, Blake or herself, for letting him talk her into doing something she didn't want to do, and she was afraid she was taking it out on Isadora. When they got to Isadora's gate, Kat put her hand on Isadora's lightly and gave her a weak smile as if to say she was sorry. "Good night, then, Isadora Crow."

"Good night, Kat Van Tassel. We should do this again sometime."

The words took Kat by surprise and made her realize how very much she'd like to see Isadora again.

Kat did her best to banish Isadora from her thoughts and focus on reading the diary. She felt warm at last snuggled in bed in her red fuzzy pj's. All she had wanted that day was some time to herself, and at last she had it, so she was going to spend it as she wished, reading the first Katrina's diary as her mother had asked her to.

FIVE

THE DIARY OF KATRINA VAN TASSEL

ICHABOD CRANE

I can't imagine that arrogant prat Brom thinks I'm going to marry him, especially after that wretched display. Then again, if it weren't for his childish behavior, I might not have met Mr. Crane that very day.

Still fuming after her argument with Brom, Katrina hastily and angrily made her way down Sleepy Hollow Road, accidentally knocking into someone who was headed in the opposite direction. "Oh!" She dropped her books in surprise. "Excuse me," she said, embarrassed. She scrambled, trying to pick them all up, but they kept falling from the haphazard piles, making her more agitated every time the books fell into the road again.

"Not at all, miss. Excuse me," said a voice she didn't recognize. When she looked up, she saw a young man she hadn't seen before. He was dressed in an impeccably natty suit, and a gentleman's hat that he tipped when he introduced himself to her. He had the most endearing yet goofy smile she had ever seen, and suddenly she wasn't feeling angry anymore.

"Hello, Miss . . ." he said, giving her a cue to introduce herself with a dramatic flair. He looked as if he were frozen mid-hat-tipping, like he had been made into a statue by a gorgon.

"Van Tassel," she said, smiling at the handsome but gangly man with overly large ears, releasing him from the gorgon's spell.

"Hello, Miss Van Tassel, I am Ichabod Crane," he said, returning his hat to his head and flashing his awkward smile again. "It's a pleasure to meet you." He leaned down to pick up her books.

"Thank you, Mr. Crane," she said, reaching out for them, but he didn't hand them over.

"You have wonderful taste in literature, Miss Van Tassel; this one is a particular favorite." He picked up the Lord Byron along with the last of Katrina's other books, and held the large stack with ease in the crook of his long gangly arm. He was so unlike the other men in Sleepy Hollow, and he was particularly different from Brom.

"What brings you to Sleepy Hollow?" she asked, feeling awkward that she was gawking at this man who seemed to have been deposited in Sleepy Hollow by some sort of supernatural means to lift her spirits when she was feeling particularly down.

"I have traveled from Connecticut to be installed as the new schoolmaster here in Sleepy Hollow." He tipped his hat again with a dramatic flourish that almost made Katrina giggle. She found him humorous and enchanting at the same time. And here she was disheveled, and probably red-faced with anger.

There was something charming yet bumbling about this man, with his too-long arms and legs, and elongated features, and an undeniable uniqueness about him that seemed to disarm her. "I do believe I have my work cut out for me as schoolmaster, Miss Van Tassel. I have a deep abiding fear that not everyone in Sleepy Hollow is so well-read as you. Were you educated outside of Sleepy Hollow, then?" he asked, looking straight into her blue eyes. She liked this man, and the way he chose his words.

"No, sir. I was taught by my governess. Though reading is my passion." She suddenly worried she was talking too much. Her mama would never approve of her talking with a man she hadn't been properly introduced to in this way, about her *passions* or anything else for that matter.

"It's refreshing to see someone in a town such as Sleepy Hollow who strives to enrich themself. I was worried I would be surrounded by nothing but bumpkins thrashing and railing against their education."

Katrina laughed.

"That very well may be the case, Mr. Crane. Sleepy Hollowians are a simple people, and I dare say you will have your hands full."

"Oh, I have my ways of reining in the rowdy boys, Miss Van Tassel." He looked down at the stack of Katrina's books that he was still holding.

"Oh! I'm sorry. Mr. Crane, please let me take those from you," she said, taking her books. She wanted to stay and talk with him some more, but she could see from his body language he was eager to get down the path.

"I would offer to carry your books home for you, but it seems we are heading in divergent directions, and I mustn't be late, Miss Van Tassel." He bowed to Katrina with another attempt at gentlemanly gesticulation. Katrina couldn't suppress her giggle this time, and not just because she thought he was funny, but because she couldn't help but feel a wee bit taken with this dashing young man.

"I do hope we cross paths again, Mr. Crane," she said, feeling bold and waving with her free hand as she continued down the Sleepy Hollow path. "I bid you a good day!"

"It's almost evening, Miss Van Tassel," he called out, pointing to the sky. "See, twilight is quickly descending into darkness." She looked up and saw Crane was right, the golden hour was almost over. Her parents were going to be furious with her if she wasn't home before dark.

"Please excuse me for rushing off, then. Mr. Crane, I mustn't be caught out after dark, and neither should you! You would do well to get to your destination without delay." She began hurrying down the road, adding in haste, "Good evening, Mr. Crane, and please do be careful on Sleepy Hollow Road."

"Good evening, Miss Van Tassel," he said, whistling as he made his way down the road behind her without a care in the world.

‿

Katrina felt a pang of guilt on her way home. She wished she hadn't rushed off like that, and she felt she really should have warned Mr. Crane about the Headless Horseman. He was new to town and probably didn't know its history. She would hate if poor Mr. Crane had an encounter with the Horseman. She couldn't stop thinking about him being terrorized on Sleepy Hollow Road, while images of Mr. Crane's head rolling down the path filled her mind. She could hardly breathe when she finally made her way home, dropping her books by the front door with a loud thump.

"Katrina!" Regina, Katrina's mother, stood in the vestibule nearest the arched entrance to the dining room. "Pick those books up at once, and get yourself upstairs and dressed for dinner! Your father will be home any moment," she said. "Home right before dark as usual, I see, and covered in dust. I don't know what you get up to while you're out all day, Katrina. I just don't know." Regina shook her head.

"I'm sorry, Mama, but it wasn't my fault. I ran into the new schoolmaster on the road. Mr. Crane is his name. It looks as though he just arrived to town today," Katrina said, making her way to the staircase.

"Schoolmaster, you say?" Katrina's mother looked intrigued. "Where is he from?" she asked, straightening her apron and fussing over her hair, as if this new man about town was going to walk in and find her in a state not befitting company.

"Connecticut, Mama! He seems so worldly, well educated, and so well-read." Katrina smiled as she remembered her conversation with Mr. Crane. It was refreshing to talk with someone who didn't think she was childish for reading.

"Well, I should hope he is well educated, Katrina, seeing that he is to be the schoolmaster!" said her mother, still fussing over her appearance.

"He's not just well educated, Mama, but also so well spoken. There's something different about him." Her mind drifted back to her meeting with Mr. Crane, hoping he didn't meet an ill fate on Sleepy Hollow Road. She felt silly for running off like she had, but she was afraid her family would be angry with her if she came home after dark, and especially for talking to a man she didn't know.

At that moment, her father, Baltus, walked in the front door looking amused by something, and couldn't wait to share it with them. "Good evening, my beauties! I just met the strangest young man on the road, a gangly scarecrow-looking fella, his clothes hung on him like he was a living skeleton! Mr. Crow, I think he said his name was." He glanced down at Katrina's stack of books by the door. "Katrina, why do you take so many books out on your walks? It looks like you're to be the next schoolmaster, and not Mr. Crow."

"Mr. Crane, darling. His name is Mr. Crane. Did you know we were to have a new schoolmaster in town?" she asked, pointing down at her husband's dirty boots, her gentle reminder that he should take them off. Baltus chuckled as he kicked off his boots, not noticing one of them had gotten mud on Katrina's books.

"Of course I knew, dear, but I hardly thought it was worth mentioning, and now that I've laid eyes on the poor pasty fellow, I'm even more convinced there is no place for him in Sleepy Hollow."

"Papa! You put your filthy boots on my books!"

"All right, calm down, Katrina," her mother said. "If you didn't leave them on the floor, that wouldn't happen. And, Baltus, put your boots away. Since the two of you decided to stride in right before dinner with no time to make yourselves presentable, why don't you quickly wash up and then meet me in the dining room before the food gets cold, and we will finish this conversation over dinner." Regina eyed her husband with a scolding look, likely upset he hadn't told her about the headmaster. Not much happened in Sleepy Hollow, and news like this was not the sort of thing you forgot to tell your wife.

Baltus sighed comically as he watched his wife totter off to the kitchen. "Is your mother in a tizzy over this new schoolmaster? Great Hollow's Ghost, help us. By this time tomorrow, I imagine every housewife in Sleepy Hollow will have invited him to dinner," he said, chuckling to himself.

Katrina and her father quickly washed up and went directly into the dining room as Regina requested. The one thing you didn't do in the Van Tassel home was show up late for dinner. The dining room table was laden with a roasted chicken stuffed with olives, garlic, and shallots alongside a large bowl of rosemary potatoes and another with buttered carrots seasoned with dill, and of course there was plenty of freshly baked bread, which Baltus usually ate in great amounts.

Katrina's mother placed a large jug of spiced wine in front of Baltus at the head of the table, and then took the seat at the other end. Katrina customarily sat to her mother's right and was eyeing the pumpkin tarts on the sideboard, realizing the annual Harvest Ball was almost upon them. Soon her mother would be in a proper tizzy preparing for the ball. She and her father would have to be sure not to test her mother's patience as they had this evening, or else Regina would unleash *the harvest wrath*, as her father called it.

Katrina couldn't remember an occasion in which her mother hadn't set a beautiful table. The dining room looked delightful. Her mother had lit candles and placed autumn-colored flowers in the center of the large wooden table, which was draped with a red tablecloth that matched their velvet curtains.

"Come on now, tuck in, dinner is getting cold," said Regina, making Baltus laugh again. Katrina loved the sound of her father's laugh; it was so deep and gravelly, and almost jolly.

"Your dinners never get cold, Regina. You are bestowed with housewifery witchcraft to keep everything searing hot no matter how long it takes Katrina and me to make it to the table." He winked at Katrina and her mother.

"Oh, stop it, Baltus! You know I don't dabble in such things." Regina poured herself some of the spiced wine from the jug that Baltus had just handed to her.

"So, you met our new Mr. Crow, then," Baltus said, heaping large portions of small golden potatoes onto his plate.

"No, dear, it was Katrina who met *Mr. Crane*, on Sleepy Hollow Road while he was making his way into town."

Baltus raised his eyebrow at Katrina. "And how did you find him, my daughter? Did his bulbous Adam's apple distract you as it did me?" he asked, now piling his plate with carrots. Katrina's father was a hulking man, over six feet in height, massively built from working on their farm, and his appetite was enormous.

"I thought he was most intriguing, Papa. He seems like he will make a fine schoolmaster," she said, putting some roasted chicken on her plate, making sure to take extra portions of the olives and garlic, which were her favorite parts of the dish.

"Well, if you ask me, I don't see why we've engaged

a schoolmaster. Most families need their boys to work their farms; they can't be sending them off to school, especially when the crops come in." Baltus was slapping his knife on his bread over and over as he spread butter in great amounts, and Katrina imagined it was Mr. Crane's face he saw as he did so. She could see he had already decided to dislike him, and when her papa didn't like someone, he usually didn't change his mind. At least he was being funny about it.

"And what about the girls, Papa? Can they be spared? Or do they need to stay home and help their mothers?" said Katrina, feeling annoyed with her father.

"You know very well that most young girls are kept home to help their families, but you received an excellent education, Katrina; you have no cause to complain." He took a sip of his spiced wine, splashing a bit on his beard.

"It wasn't a real education, though, was it, Papa? It was from a governess. I would have liked to go to a proper school. I still would." She cast a look at her mother to see what she would say. This had been a sore subject between Katrina and her family, and as much as she hated to shift the jovial mood in the room, it was something she felt strongly about.

"We've already discussed this, Katrina," Regina said. "We won't have you going off to school, and that's final."

This was a topic Katrina brought up often, but she could never convince her parents to relent. She desperately wanted to go away to school, but nothing she said seemed to convince her parents to let her go.

Then, suddenly, Regina got a glint in her eye, as she often did when she felt she had come up with a brilliant idea. "*However*, if you'd like us to engage Mr. Crane to tutor you in some additional subjects, perhaps something can be arranged. I'd love to have this young man over to dinner anyway," said her mother, smiling at Katrina.

Katrina knew her mother was trying to make up for being so stalwartly against her going away to school. And though it wasn't a victory, at least she would have the opportunity to talk with someone who valued education and she had something in common with.

"Oh, Mama, really? Do you mean it? What night will you invite him? What do you think I should wear? Oh, and I must find my Voltaire, I think Mr. Crane would appreciate him. He seems like the sort of man who would grasp his wit."

Baltus narrowed his eyes at his daughter as she gushed.

"And, Mama, how far along are you on that new dress you're making for me? Do you think I could wear it when he comes to dinner?" Katrina's eyes were filled with excitement.

But this was all too much for Baltus. He had finally lost his patience, and slammed his overly buttered bread onto his plate. "Now listen here, no one said we were having this fool of an upstart over to dinner! He has an ill-favored look about him, Regina. I don't like him. What would we talk about? I like to relax with my family after a long day at work, not entertain people I have no care to keep company with." Katrina's mother set her wine goblet onto the table with a thud of frustration.

"Of course we are having him over to dinner, Baltus. When have you ever known the Van Tassels not to open their home and be neighborly? And yes, Katrina, your dress will be ready in time. Now both of you, calm down and eat your dinner."

Katrina gave her mother a brilliant smile, because she knew that was the end of it. Regina had spoken.

"Oh, thank you, Mama," she said, dashing out of her

seat and rushing over to give her mother a kiss. "May I please be excused? I wanted to find that book and reread it before I see Mr. Crane. I want to have something for us to talk about the next time I see him," she said, making her mother smile and shake her head.

"Go on, then, Katrina," she said, laughing as Katrina ran upstairs.

"I don't like seeing Katrina's head so turned, Regina. I don't like it one bit. She's promised to Brom."

"Don't worry, Baltus. This young man is a passing fancy, and if he isn't, and it turns out they are well suited, then you will have to get used to the idea."

Katrina's father pushed himself away from the table, stood up, and went to the fireplace.

"Baltus, don't smoke that pipe in the house! If you're going to smoke, then do it on the porch."

"I'll smoke in my own house if I want to, Regina!" he said grumpily.

"Don't snap at me, Baltus, just because you're angry at Katrina. I know you like Brom, but anyone can see they've been drifting apart. She's not like other girls in Sleepy Hollow, dear, and if she'd be happier with someone like this Mr. Crane, then who are we to stand in her way?"

Katrina, who had been listening from the banister upstairs, was surprised.

"So, you're going to marry her off to the first gangly twit who waltzes into town? We're her parents! I'm sorry, Regina, but we can't have someone the likes of Mr. Crow running this farm! Brom is the man for Katrina! I know it, and you know it! We've all known it since they were small!" Katrina's mother laughed and patted Baltus on the arm.

"His name is Mr. Crane, dear. And we're getting ahead of ourselves, don't you think? But let's just say for the sake of argument Katrina does marry this school-master, who is to say they can't hire someone to oversee the farm?"

Baltus, who was getting more red-faced by the moment, lit his pipe with a look that dared his wife to say something about it. "I don't know, Regina. I just don't know," he said, blowing out the smoke in large white plumes.

"I know you like Brom, dear. And who knows, maybe this infatuation with Mr. Crane will scare Brom into being the suitor Katrina deserves. Or it may make our daughter realize that Brom is the one for her. Let's just see how it plays out. But in the meantime, you realize we are having him over to dinner." She patted him on his massive arm again with her tiny hand.

"Yes, dear," he said. "And I'll finish smoking on the porch," he said, looking defeated.

"Thank you, dear," she said, giving him a light kiss on his cheek.

"You never know, perhaps this Mr. Crow won't live up to her expectations," said Baltus.

"His name is Mr. Crane, dear. And I wouldn't count on it."

Katrina stood from where she was eavesdropping by the stairs. Satisfied that she had won this family argument, she went off to find her Voltaire.

SIX

THE DIARY OF KATRINA VAN TASSEL

ENTER, MR. CROW

Katrina's mother was busy in the kitchen preparing the evening meal when Katrina came scrambling in acting as if she was being chased down by the devil himself. "Mama! Look at my dress! Right here," she said, spinning around in a panic to show her a pucker at the back. "I can't wear it like this; what am I going to do?" Regina and Madeline, the woman who helped Katrina's mother in the kitchen on occasion, looked up from what they were doing and frowned.

"Come here so I can take a better look," Regina said, inspecting the back of Katrina's dress. "Oh, this is fine, Katrina. Wear your red sash around your waist; it will hide that pucker and it will look beautiful with the dress. Go back upstairs and put it on; then come here and I'll make sure it's doing the trick," she said, turning to continue rolling the dough for the pies she was baking as Katrina ran back upstairs.

"It seems Miss Katrina is smitten with the new schoolmaster. Have things gone sour between her and Brom?" asked Madeline as she continued rolling the other piece of dough.

"Oh, I don't know. I think it's just a harmless fascination. He's new, and worldly, you know how it is. We rarely if ever have a new person in town," said Regina.

Katrina could hear her mother and Madeline talking from her bedroom at the top of the stairs. Which was why on occasion she would leave her door open, so she could eavesdrop when she needed to.

"From what I hear, there hasn't been a night that Mr. Crane has had to fend for himself. He's been invited to every home in all of Sleepy Hollow, and stuffed to the gills by every housewife in the county. I suppose they just want to get a proper look at him to see if he'd be a good match for their daughters, and from the sound of it, it seems Mr. Crane doesn't mind," said Madeline, laughing. There wasn't anything that happened in Sleepy Hollow that Madeline didn't know about. "The Van Irvings said Mr. Crane has an exceedingly large appetite, which surprises me, he's such a slim man. Mrs. Van Irving said he had indeed eaten not only seconds but thirds and still he had room for two slices of pie, stuffing himself like a Christmas goose!" she said, making Katrina's mother laugh.

Katrina shook her head as she listened to them, but started to worry. The last thing she wanted was Madeline spreading it around town she had eyes for Mr. Crane. She didn't want Brom's feelings hurt, especially when she didn't completely understand how she felt. It was really just as her mother said. She was excited to meet someone new and different, and it didn't hurt that they had a great deal in common.

"Well, perhaps he's accepting all these invitations due to his love of food, and not because he's shopping around for a bride," said Regina, laughing.

Whatever the reason, Crane had accepted their invitation to dinner this evening, and Katrina knew her mother wasn't about to leave her dinner guest wanting. She had made a roast beef, as well as a roasted chicken stuffed with olives and garlic, pork chops stuffed with herbs, her usual golden potatoes and buttered carrots, as well as brussels sprouts with bacon, green beans with slivered almonds, and a few extra loaves of bread. Not to mention three different pies: pumpkin, apple, and cherry. It seemed her mother was determined to send Ichabod home stuffed to the gills as well. Some months later, Katrina's mother told her daughter what happened next, because when she heard the knock at the door, she panicked and slammed the door of her bedroom closed for fear Crane would see her before she was ready.

Katrina's mother was funny when she told her the story. It seemed the moment Regina finished pinching the edges of the pies and was about to get them into the oven that she heard the knock at the door. She wasn't expecting their guest for another hour at least, so she assumed it was a neighbor. She took off her apron, wiping her hands on it as she made her way to the door, and found a tall gangly man standing there holding a bunch of wildflowers in his left hand.

"Well, hello there, you must be Mr. Crow—excuse me, I mean Mr. Crane. I am Mrs. Van Tassel; won't you please come in?" she said, looking at the stately grandfather clock that stood in the small vestibule to make sure she hadn't lost track of time. Mr. Crane was exceedingly early, and that was something Katrina's mother couldn't abide.

"Good evening, Mrs. Van Tassel, so pleased to meet you at last," said the lanky young man in his too-baggy black suit. "I see now where Katrina gets her striking good looks." Crane walked into the vestibule and looked around, clearly taken by the size of the Van Tassel home.

"Won't you please follow me to the library? I'm afraid Mr. Van Tassel isn't home yet and Katrina is still upstairs. May I offer you some sherry while you wait?" she said, motioning to the library.

It was a charming room with dark wood furnishings that were beautifully engraved. The main feature was the bookshelves that lined the walls, which were carved to look like gnarled and sprawling oak trees with the numerous books nestled within their trunks and branches. The fireplace was equally impressive due to its massive size, almost dwarfing the pair of cozy chairs that sat on either side facing the hearth. Across the room was a small window nook for reading, with embroidered pillows for comfort, and nearby was a large display case with several of Mrs. Van Tassel's treasures and family keepsakes.

"Thank you, Mrs. Van Tassel. I'm afraid I have arrived too early." Katrina's mother later remarked that she could see Mr. Crane was impressed with the room even though he didn't say so. She had a fondness for this room and loved that it was her own grandfather who had carved the bookshelves himself.

"Not at all, Mr. Crane. Please make yourself comfortable here by the fire. The sherry and glasses are on the mantel; please help yourself while I go check on Katrina," she said, skirting out of the room.

Katrina knew that promptness was a virtue her mother admired, but she thought arriving too early was just as rude as arriving late. But she told Katrina she was sure Crane must have been as excited about that evening as Katrina was, and she could hardly blame him for that, and she had a feeling he was there for more than her legendary good cooking.

Thankfully, Katrina's mother had already been dressed for dinner and had finished up most of the preparations for the meal before he arrived. If he had arrived just a bit earlier, Katrina knew her mother would be very cross, and that was not how she wanted to start off their evening.

She had admitted later to Katrina that she thought there was indeed a scarecrow quality about the young man, and his clothes did hang off him in an almost-comical fashion. She frankly wondered what her daughter saw in him. Perhaps it was his intellect that had her so intrigued. She had to admit Brom didn't share Katrina's love of reading, and she wondered if there was much for the two of them to talk about.

She quickly went upstairs and knocked on Katrina's bedroom door, entering when she heard her say "Come in" from the other side. Katrina was standing in front of the mirror checking to see if the sash had covered the pucker as Regina had hoped. Her mother couldn't help but grimace at the state of Katrina's room, in complete disarray due to her nervousness getting ready that evening. But it didn't account for the books scattered everywhere she looked, or her desk covered in stacks of her writings, or the ink splotches all over the fine wood. Kat was thankful her mother didn't remark on the state of her room, but rather turned her attentions to her dress, because Katrina was still not convinced it would do.

"Oh my, Katrina you look beautiful. And that sash

covers the pucker perfectly," Regina said, making one final adjustment and straightening out the sash for her.

"Thank you, Mama. You did a beautiful job on my dress." It was a deep red velvet, and the bright red satin sash tied at her waist was the perfect accent.

"Here, Katrina, let's pull some of your hair away from your face," said Regina, taking the hairbrush off Katrina's vanity.

"Thank you, Mama. You don't think Madeline will gossip about our having Mr. Crane over for dinner?" she said, looking at herself in the mirror as her mother fussed over her hair.

"I wouldn't worry about it, dear. Everyone in the county has had Mr. Crane for dinner; why shouldn't we?" she said, tying the bow that held Katrina's hair back. "There, you look perfect, my darling."

Katrina hugged her mother, kissing her on each of her cheeks.

"Thank you, Mama, for making me this dress, and for having Mr. Crane over to dinner. I know Papa doesn't approve."

"Oh, don't you worry about your father, Katrina. You leave him to me. Why don't we go downstairs so I can check on dinner. You will find Mr. Crane sitting in the library next to the fire. If he hasn't already poured himself a glass of sherry, please offer him some, and I will be in to join you shortly."

"Do I really look all right, Mama?"

Regina laughed again, finding herself hoping Mr. Crane was there for more than a good meal.

"You look lovely; you just need one more final touch," she said, taking Katrina's gold locket from her vanity and fastening it around her neck. "There, now you look perfect; go down and entertain your Mr. Crane until your father comes home. Now let's get downstairs. I'm not sure how your father will feel walking into the house and finding the dreaded 'Mr. Crow' lurking in the library unattended."

"Mama! He's not *my* Mr. Crane!" Katrina's face turned a shade closely resembling the red sash on her dress. Regina grasped both of her daughter's hands and kissed her on the cheek.

"Calm yourself, dear. It's just dinner." Katrina kissed her back and went bounding down the stairs. It made Regina laugh that Katrina was still very much a girl in some ways even though she was a young lady of eighteen. Later, Katrina's mother told her that she had originally indulged this idea of Mr. Crane because she knew if she discouraged Katrina's interest in him it would only make Katrina more infatuated, but she was slowly starting to understand what she saw in the strange young man, and her heart felt light seeing her daughter so happy. Besides, she hated the idea of Katrina leaving Sleepy Hollow, and if the only way to keep her home was to have her settle down with the likes of Mr. Crane, then so be it. She was almost thankful this oddball schoolmaster had come to town; she had become increasingly afraid Katrina would go off to the city in search of a partner who shared her interests. This way, she and Katrina would both have what they wanted. She and Baltus would just have to get used to the idea of a very different sort of son-in-law than they imagined if this turned out to be more than a passing fancy. Mr. Crane couldn't have been more different than Brom, and Regina had to wonder if that wasn't why Katrina was so infatuated with him. They had always taken it for granted Katrina and Brom would be married, and Regina felt there was a part of her that hoped that would still happen. She had a hard time imagining

Katrina throwing over Brom for a young man she had just met, but she supposed they would just have to see what happened.

Regina made her way to the vestibule quickly after checking on dinner, hoping she would be able to intercept Baltus before he came across Mr. Crane and Katrina in the library. She knew he didn't approve of Crane, and she feared if he was rude to him it would just make Katrina want him more. She felt the smarter thing for Baltus to do was have a nice long chat with Brom, man to man, and give him some advice on how to make Katrina happier. Because that was what Regina wanted, her daughter's happiness, no matter whom she decided to marry.

SEVEN

THE FLAMING PUMPKIN

K at looked up from Katrina's diary and noticed it was well into the night. She had been reading since she got home from the cemetery. She couldn't wait to see what happened next, but she was too exhausted to continue. Baltus and Regina made her laugh; they reminded her of her own parents. There were a lot of things about Katrina's life that reminded her of her own. It was uncanny, really. Maybe it was because she was so tired, combined with everything that happened earlier that night at the cemetery, but she had the strangest sensation that she was living Katrina's life and not her own. She saw them on similar paths, and it frightened her.

She wondered if it was too late to text Isadora. She picked up her phone and saw Isadora had texted her back at midnight. Blake hadn't texted. She didn't mind; she was still angry with him and didn't know what she wanted to say to him anyway. For all he knew, she and Isadora were lying dead in the cemetery with their heads lopped off, victims of the Headless Horseman. She read Isadora's text.

Isadora
12:00
It's the Witching Hour and all is well.

Kat wished Isadora wasn't so overawed by all this Sleepy Hollow nonsense, but for some reason, it didn't annoy her, at least not too much. She wasn't like the Sleepy Hollow Boys, or the kids in her classes—she seemed genuinely interested in the supernatural, and she wasn't just trying to be cool. Isadora was the first person she met that she thought she could become friends with who wasn't one of Blake's friends, and it felt exciting to have a friend that was just hers.

Kat
2:00
Are you awake?

Isadora
2:01
Watching a movie. What are you doing?

Kat
2:02
I was reading Katrina's diary

Isadora
2:03
YOU HAVE HER DIARY? That's crazy!

Kat
2:04
My mom gave it to me. I didn't
expect it to be so interesting

Isadora
2:05
Is it at all like the legend? Did she write about
Ichabod Crane or the Headless Horseman?

Kat
2:06
I haven't gotten that far yet. She's just
met Ichabod, and he's coming over
to dinner for the first time. Her dad
hates him! Hahaha. I want to read how
the dinner goes but I'm too tired

Isadora
2:07
Of course you are, it was a crazy night. I'd
love to read it, too, if it's not too weird

Kat

2:09

It's not weird. What's weird is how
much my life is like Katrina's

2:10

You never said what movie you're watching

Isadora

2:10

Gaslight. It's an old Ingrid Bergman movie

Kat

2:11

Oh! She's Isabella Rossellini's mother, right?
I think I read that when I was reading about
David Lynch. Do you like his movies?

Isadora

2:13

I do! He's one of my favorite filmmakers.
You're literally the only person in Sleepy
Hollow I've met who knows his work!
Then again, I just moved here lol

Kat

2:14

Yeah, there aren't many people at our school
who like stuff like that. Do you want to meet
for coffee or something tomorrow? I can tell
you what I've read in the diary so far

Isadora

2:15

Totally! Where should we meet?

> **Kat**
> *2:16*
> Do you know where the Flaming Pumpkin is?

Isadora
2:17
No, but I can find it. What time?

> **Kat**
> *2:18*
> How's noon?

Isadora
2:19
Perfect! See you then!

Kat was happy it didn't seem like Isadora was still upset with her, but she still felt bad for everything that had happened that night and for how she had treated her as they walked home. She would tell her tomorrow that she was sorry. She felt like she spent her life saying sorry—to her parents, and to Blake, and now Isadora. She felt like she was always unintentionally hurting people, and she wondered if Blake was right, and perhaps she really was a selfish person.

⌣

Kat decided to walk to the café to meet Isadora the next day. As she passed the stately and venerable town

clock with its sinister-looking scarecrow that seemed
to be smiling at her, it made her laugh. The town was
getting geared up for the Autumn Festival, and the
decorations were in abundance. She thought the town
was beautiful as it was; she didn't think it needed all
the decorations; there was a spookiness to it without all
the hanging ghosts, legions of jack-o'-lanterns, and of
course the figure of the Headless Horseman astride his
horse at the covered bridge so tourists could stop and
take a selfie beside it. This was a town of contradictions
in Kat's view: on one hand treating their history with
reverence to the point of delirium, and on the other
exploiting it to pander to the people who came from
the city for the festival. As much as she hated the old-
fashioned notions of the people who lived there, she
admired how beautifully preserved Sleepy Hollow was.
She loved the old stone and brick buildings, but most
of all she loved the burnt orange and red leaves that
dominated the landscape this time of year.

When she got to the café, she smirked at the
large wooden sign that hung above the door. It was
an enormous flaming jack-o'-lantern that looked as if
it was hurtling above the doorway. It drove her batty
how everything in Sleepy Hollow was, well, Sleepy

Hollow–themed, but she had a feeling Isadora would like this café. It was one of Kat's favorite places.

A brass bell rang as she opened the door, and she scanned the room to see if Isadora was there. Her heart sank a little when she didn't see her, and she worried she had changed her mind. She should have texted that she was sorry last night.

She couldn't decide if she should order something before she found a table or wait for Isadora to get there—if she was showing up at all. The café was empty aside from the barista, Raven, who didn't look a thing like her name suggested. She looked more like *a Katrina* than Kat did, with her light blond hair, peaches-and-cream complexion, and bubbly, friendly personality. That is, she was friendly and bubbly with everyone except Kat. For some reason, Raven didn't seem to like her much. It didn't bother Kat; she was used to people treating her strangely. It came with being a Katrina. People her age either worshiped Katrinas or hated them. Her mom said it was jealousy, but Kat didn't understand what there was to be jealous of. She'd give anything to be free of the legacy that bound her to Sleepy Hollow.

Kat decided she would claim her favorite spot, a cozy corner near the stone fireplace that was adorned with ceramic jack-o'-lanterns, with rubber bats that hung overhead. She sat in the antique brown leather armchair that was across from an old-fashioned red-velvet couch. Between the two was a small round wood table.

Most places in Sleepy Hollow were like this, filled with antiques, and perpetually decorated for Halloween even when it wasn't festival time. But she loved this café with its vintage red rugs, dark woodwork, and even the kitschy Halloween decorations. What she loved most, though, were the old horror movie posters that hung on the walls, a holdover from when the café was originally a movie theater. She especially loved the silent film posters. In her corner were framed posters of *The Phantom of the Opera*, *Metropolis*, and Jean Cocteau's *Beauty and the Beast*; the latter of course wasn't a silent, but it was one of her most beloved films. This was one of her favorite places to sit and read aside from the Oldest Tree. She used to love going there with Blake; they would sit for hours just talking, but lately he was only interested in hanging out with the other Sleepy Hollow Boys, ghost hunting, or whatever they were up to. He didn't want to hear about her favorite movies anymore, the stories she wanted to write, and he refused to talk with her about how she wanted to go away to college. Maybe they had just been together for so long there was nothing left to talk about.

As she was looking at the *Beauty and the Beast* poster, she mused over how many times she had watched that film. She felt like Belle, perpetually trapped in antiquation and gloom with a beast. The ending used to cheer her; Belle saw the man beneath the Beast's cursed visage, reached in, found his beautiful soul, and brought it out for all to see. But with Blake, she found it harder to see that glimmer of the person she had once loved so dearly: the sweet boy who protected her, went on adventures with her in Sleepy Hollow Woods, or quietly sat next to her as they read their favorite books. She sometimes wondered why they were still together with so little left in common. She had tried to talk with him about it, but he would dismiss her saying she had changed, that she didn't know how to be happy anymore, and she wondered if he was right. She wasn't happy. Perhaps if she was, Blake would be, too, and things would go back to the way they were.

Just then she heard the brass bell ring, and she looked up and saw it was Isadora. Her long black hair hung straight down to her shoulders, and she wore a black vintage slip as a dress layered with a long lace sweater, a vintage velvet coat with silver buttons, a long gray-and-black scarf, and knee-high black boots. She had a large black bag hanging off her shoulder, and her phone was in her hand. She stopped and took photos of the bats hanging from the ceiling and then slipped her phone into her bag. When she looked up, she saw Kat, who smiled at her.

"Hi! I'm so happy you texted me last night," she said as she made her way over to where Kat was sitting. Kat couldn't stop smiling at her.

"I was worried you were upset with me about everything that happened at the cemetery," Kat said. The firelight brought out the gold flecks in Isadora's brown eyes, and they looked hauntingly beautiful, and Kat suddenly felt her face get hot, like she was blushing.

"Honestly, I was afraid you were upset with me," Isadora said as she took off her coat and put it over the back of the red-velvet couch, set her bag down next to her, and took a seat. "I hope I didn't make things worse. I know you don't need me to stand up for you, but I couldn't help it. Blake's friends were being awful."

"I wasn't upset with you. I'm upset with myself and with Blake. I'm sorry if I took it out on you, and I'm sorry I went along with their stupid plan to summon Katrina. I didn't realize it would frighten you so much."

"Don't worry about it. Did you order coffee yet? What's good here?" she asked, digging around in her bag for her wallet. Kat thought Isadora looked a little nervous.

"Everyone swears by the pumpkin spice, but I'm a cappuccino girl. And by the way, I'm not upset you stood up for me. I thought it was kinda rad actually," Kat said. She wished she was sitting on the couch with Isadora.

"Is the foam thick, or do they make them all milky like a latte? And I'm happy you're not mad at me. I have a tendency to say what I feel even when it's not appropriate," she said, finding her wallet. It was in the shape of a book that said *Magic Spells* on the spine.

"I love your wallet," Kat said, taking hers out of her purse. "Look!" She showed her she had one that was almost the same, but it said *Adventure Stories* with an image of a hot-air balloon. They both laughed, and Kat realized that she was feeling nervous now, too.

"That's awesome! So is the foam thick?" Isadora stood, her wallet in hand; she looked like she wanted a reason to excuse herself. Kat didn't understand why they were both so nervous.

"Oh, sorry, yeah. I don't drink them any other way." Kat noticed Raven was eyeing them from the counter.

"Cool. What size do you want? Do I order at the counter?" All she was doing was standing there, a perfectly ordinary thing to do, but Kat loved looking at her. She seemed so comfortable in her own skin, so sure of herself.

"Yeah, but I was going to treat you," said Kat, reaching for her bag.

"Don't be silly; I'll be right back," said Isadora, flashing her beautiful dark eyes.

Kat didn't understand why she felt so awkward; maybe it was because she had the sense that Isadora was her own person and didn't shy away from sharing her opinions, while Kat sometimes felt too shy to share how she was feeling (unless she was arguing with her parents). Whatever the reason, she wanted to get over it. She liked Isadora and wanted to get to know her better; the last thing she wanted to do was make her feel uncomfortable by being an awkward mess. To distract herself, she took the diary out of her purse and started reading. She saw a shadow pass over her as she was reading and thought Isadora was already back. She looked up and didn't see anyone there. No one else was in the café, but she could swear someone was standing right in front her. She felt a chill, even though she was sitting right next to the fire. The same chill she felt at the cemetery, but not as overwhelming. She scanned the room, feeling as though someone was watching her, and she couldn't help but feel a little scared.

"Hey, are you okay? It looks like you've seen a ghost," Isadora said, sitting back down on the couch. Kat wanted to say she almost felt like she had, just the quickest glimpse of one, but she knew she was just worked up after everything that had happened at the cemetery. This always happened when she was really stressed, all her old anxieties and fears creeping back up to the surface. She told herself it was just a trick of the light. *Ghosts don't exist.*

"Raven said she is going to bring our drinks over when she's done making them."

"She must like you, she usually just screeches my name as loudly as she can when she's done making my coffee even if I'm the only one in here. She's literally nice to everyone but me," she said, laughing.

Isadora smiled cheekily. "She probably has a crush on you."

That hadn't even occurred to Kat. "Oh, I don't know. Do you really think so?" asked Kat, feeling even more nervous and wanting to change the subject. "She probably has a crush on *you*," Kat said, scanning Isadora. "Is that a Poe scarf?" Isadora's scarf had an image of a raven with passages from "The Raven" by Edgar Allan Poe printed on it.

"It is! Don't tell me you have one, too, but with Jane Austen quotes," she said, laughing. (The fact was Kat did, and almost wore it because it was a chilly day, but she didn't want Isadora to think she was a dork.) "I don't think Raven has a crush on me; she probably just likes my scarf. She was telling me she is really into Poe."

"Have you seen that video of Vincent Price reading 'The Raven'? It's amazing," Kat said, changing the subject again.

"Oh my god, I love that video! I listen to it every year right before Halloween. I love Vincent Price."

"Me too! I also always listen to the original radio play of *The War of the Worlds* by Orson Welles right before Halloween," said Kat, smiling. She had never met someone her age who loved this kind of stuff. For all of the Sleepy Hollow Boys' love of all things spooky, they didn't know anything about classic horror.

"Right, because it first aired the night before Halloween!" said Isadora as Raven came over with the coffees.

"Here you go, ladies," she said, looking especially grumpy. Both girls thanked her, and looked at each other like *What was that about?* as she walked away.

"I think she's jealous," said Isadora, taking a sip, her cat eyes flashing playfully.

"What do you mean?" Kat didn't understand why this girl made her feel so nervous.

"Never mind. Tell me what you've read in Katrina's diary so far."

"Right before you came back, I was reading about Ichabod poking around Katrina's house, remarking how rich her family was. You'd think that would have been a clue," she said, laughing, but Isadora didn't laugh with her. "I didn't get far in that chapter, I just skimmed it, but it looks like Katrina's dad brought Brom home to dinner."

"I can't wait to see how that goes," said Isadora, smirking, but she looked distracted.

"Is everything really okay? Are you sure you're not still upset with me about last night?"

"I'm not. It's just I need to talk with you about something, and you're not going to like it..."

"I know, you hate Blake and his friends, they were being jerks last night. They can be really weird about outsiders, you know, people who aren't from Sleepy Hollow. They'll get over it."

"I hope so." But Kat could see it was still bothering her, or at least something was, but Isadora changed the subject. "So, what else have you read so far?" she asked, kicking off her shoes and then curling her legs up on the couch.

"Nothing juicy yet, just how Katrina and Ichabod met. Her parents are really keen on her marrying Brom, but she's not feeling it, and her father hates Ichabod. Her mom seems cooler about everything, even encouraging her interest in Crane, I think mostly because she's afraid Katrina will break up with Brom and want to leave Sleepy Hollow."

"Is Ichabod as much of a creeper as he seems in the legend?" asked Isadora, still distracted. She clearly had something else on her mind, but Kat didn't want to bug her about it. That was something Kat was trying to work on. She could often tell when something was bothering someone, or when they weren't being truthful, and she hated being lied to. She found more times than not when she asked someone what was wrong, they'd say "nothing," and then she'd feel like they were lying when really what they meant to say was they didn't want to talk about it. She and Blake used to fight about this all the time. She could always tell when he was keeping something from her, and he would lie no matter how many times she asked, until she ended up feeling like she was losing her mind. She didn't want to give Isadora a reason to lie, even if it was a harmless one.

"Crane is kind of a creeper. He seems super pompous to me, like he's always putting on an act," said Kat, laughing. "But he's really funny, too, always tipping his hat, and doing all these fancy things, and making proclamations, but I guess that's how people were back then."

"I wonder why Katrina liked him so much?" asked Isadora, looking as if she was trying to imagine the Ichabod Crane Kat had just described.

"Because he was new to town and entirely different from anyone she knew. They had a lot in common," she said, feeling her cheeks get warm again. "She didn't know anyone else who loved the same things she did." Kat looked down at the diary, wondering if Isadora caught on that she was talking as much about the two of them as she was about Katrina and Ichabod.

"Kind of like us." Isadora always spoke with authority. Kat had never heard her own voice sound so small, as if she wasn't sure of herself.

"Almost exactly like us," said Kat, looking back up to meet Isadora's gaze. Kat was thrown off by how much she liked this girl, and she was sure Isadora liked her back. But what did it mean? Was she just excited to have a new friend, or was it something more?

"Want to sit on the couch with me and read what's next together?" Isadora asked, moving her purse over. And Kat knew the moment she sat next to her that she liked this girl as more than just a friend.

EIGHT

THE DIARY OF
KATRINA VAN TASSEL

THE UNEXPECTED DINNER GUEST

*I nervously made my way into the library to find
Ichabod standing near Mama's display case, looking
at the trinkets within. "Good evening, Mr. Crane,"
I said, thinking that he looked dashing in his black
suit and wondering what this evening would bring.*

~

"Good evening, Miss Van Tassel. I have had
the pleasure of dining in many homes since
I arrived to Sleepy Hollow but none so fine as
this. I daresay your family is the richest in the county,"
he said, eyeing the fine figurines, silver snuff boxes, and
candlesticks in the case.

"I wouldn't know," said Katrina, knowing full well they were. These things just weren't talked about and she was shocked Mr. Crane had said it aloud.

"Excuse my vulgarity, Miss Van Tassel. I know one shouldn't mention such things." She watched as he ran his hand along the carvings of oak tree branches on the finely crafted wooden desk near the window nook. She took this room for granted; she had grown up pulling books off these shelves, and sitting in the window seat reading for hours or just gazing at the intricate wood-work, her mind drifting to dark forests with oak trees that were alive and holding secrets of their own. She had never thought about what it must be like to see this room for the first time.

"Think nothing of it, Mr. Crane. My great-grandfather did all of these carvings." She didn't know why, but she suddenly felt nervous. All week, Ichabod had been distant. Sure, she had met him on the road, and they had a splendid conversation, but she had spent more time thinking about him than she had actually spent in his company while waiting for this evening. She had created her own version of who he was, and she wondered who she would like better, the real Mr. Crane or the one she imagined.

"Please, call me Ichabod," he said, with a wild flourish that looked as if he tipped an invisible hat. Katrina giggled. This was one of the things she found charming about him, though she was sure her father would detest it. He hated when people "put on airs," as he put it, but she felt this aspect of Mr. Crane's personality came quite naturally to him and she found it refreshing.

"I have never met a man quite like you, Ichabod," she said, quickly turning around to see who was coming into the room. It was Brom, and he pushed his way in like a great bull, still dirty from working the fields all day. He was followed closely by Katrina's mother, who had a horrified look on her face, and not just because he had tracked mud onto her fine carpets.

"Katrina, look who your father brought home for dinner," she said, looking rather uncomfortable. Katrina could tell by the look on her mother's face that Regina was as surprised as she was to see Brom. *This is going to be a disaster,* she thought.

"Now, Brom, you know better than to come into my library with dirty boots. Get yourself upstairs and washed up before dinner." Regina had her hands on her hips, but Brom's eyes were fixed on Crane. "Come on now, off with you. And tell Baltus to lend you one of his nice shirts. I'm sorry he didn't tell you we were dressing for dinner this evening."

"Well, if you expect me to come back down looking like this dandy, you'll be disappointed," said Brom, hulking in the doorway, never taking his eyes off Crane.

"Well, I think Mr. Crane looks handsome," said Katrina, giving Brom a dirty look. She hated that he was ruining their evening already. The idea that someone either not being from Sleepy Hollow or acting differently in any way was somehow an excuse to treat them this way was beyond Katrina. She knew she was already going to have her hands full with her father, but now she had to deal with Brom, too, and she was beyond annoyed and wished they could just call the entire evening off.

"When Baltus told me you were in a state over this puffed-up schoolmaster, I guess he wasn't kidding." Brom gave Crane a seething look. The notion that "outsiders" were to be distrusted was alien to Katrina. She found people who weren't from Sleepy Hollow interesting, and she was happy she and her mother were of like mind, because it was clear her mother was also getting frustrated with Brom's behavior. Katrina had to admit, however, that Brom's dislike for Mr. Crane probably went deeper than the mere fact he was new to town.

"Now, none of that, Brom!" Regina said, pointing at the doorway and firmly ushering Brom out of the room.

"Please excuse Brom, Mr. Crane, and *please* don't pay attention to what he said about my father. I'm sure he said no such thing." She was certain her face was as scarlet as the sash on her dress. And she knew for a fact her father had likely said those things. Katrina was mortified. Crane tried to pull it off like he was unfazed, but his laugh was wry.

"I've met my share of our neighbors, Miss Van Tassel, and while I find the womenfolk most pleasant, I have found that the men are, how do we say, a bit standoffish," he said, laughing again and taking a sip of his sherry and then holding up the glass to the light so he could admire the lovely etched crystal glass.

"I'm so sorry, Mr. Crane. I'm rather embarrassed, I must say," she said, still rather red-cheeked.

"I don't take offense to their remarks, dear lady; I take them as a compliment. It's understandable they would be intimidated by my intellect and worldliness. There is nothing for you to apologize for, sweet Katrina.

I hope I may call you Katrina?" he asked, taking her hand and boldly kissing it right as Regina walked into the room.

"Katrina, Mr. Crane, dinner is ready, if you could please join us in the dining room. Now!" she said curtly.

"Shall I escort you into the dining room, dear lady?" Crane put out his arm for Katrina to take, but Regina wasn't having it

"Oh, that won't be necessary, Mr. Crane. After you," said Regina, ushering him forward and out of the room ahead of them so she could whisper with Katrina alone.

"Just what are you thinking letting a young man you hardly know kiss you on the hand like that? My goodness, Katrina, you're lucky it was I who walked in and not your father."

Katrina didn't know what to say. She didn't know what she was thinking either. There was something about Crane that completely turned her head.

"I'm sorry, Mama, I promise he was being a gentleman. Mr. Crane was assuring me I needn't make apologies for Brom's rudeness."

Regina shook her head. "I don't know what your father was thinking inviting Brom. Well, I do, but never you mind. Let's just try to make the most of the evening. Oh my, I hear your Mr. Crane in there now speaking with your father and Brom. We'd better hurry and help the poor fellow out." Regina quickened her pace, Katrina following quickly behind her.

Katrina whispered, "He's not *my* Mr. Crane!" But when Katrina and her mother walked into the dining room, they found Ichabod was holding his own, even if he looked as if he was caught between two bulls deciding which would gore the poor man with their horns first.

"So, you're Mr. Crow, the new schoolmaster, then, here to teach our Sleepy Hollow boys to write and read?" said Baltus, standing at his customary spot near the fireplace about to light his pipe.

"Yes, Mr. Van Tassel, I said so when we met on Sleepy Hollow Road," said Crane with a smirk.

Baltus lit his pipe with a match and then handed the match to Brom, who was taking his pipe from his breast pocket. They almost looked like bookends, the two of them flanking either side of the hearth, two versions of the same man, one young and one middle-aged. It hadn't occurred to Katrina until that moment how much Brom favored her father, both in looks and personality.

"Here you go, my boy," said the great hulking beast of a man.

"Thank you, Baltus," Brom said, looking very at ease in the Van Tassel home. "And what about you, Crane? Care to join us for a smoke before dinner?"

Crane waved his hand as if shooing away an annoyance. "No, no, sir. I dare not offend the ladies by filling this lovely dining room with more smoke than necessary." He smiled for Regina, and Katrina was sure he was on his way to making up for his misstep in kissing her hand.

"Yes, take that outside, the both of you," Regina said, giving both of them reproving looks. "I'll send Katrina out to get you when dinner is on the table."

"Here, Mrs. Van Tassel, let me help you." Crane escorted her into the kitchen, leaving Katrina alone with her father and Brom, giving her a chance to have it out with them.

"What are you doing here, Brom? And, Papa, please do stop calling him *Mr. Crow,* you know very well his name is *Crane*! Now both of you start behaving yourselves or you can just stay outside on the porch while the civilized dine in peace."

"Since when do you talk like that, Katrina?" Brom

said. "After one evening with this lanky twit, you're talking like him? This isn't you!" The fact was, it was exactly like her, but she had somehow lost that part of herself in recent years, and spending time with a wordsmith like Crane reminded her.

"You don't know who I am, Abraham Von Brunt!" said Katrina, closing the front door on the two with a great slam. She had had enough of the both of them.

She hardly knew what to do. She was livid. She couldn't believe her father had invited Brom to dinner. Sometimes she wondered if her father wouldn't have preferred to have a son, because he always seemed to be happiest in Brom's company. She could hear the two of them laughing on the other side of the door and wondered what was so funny. She stood there for a while composing herself before she started to make her way to the kitchen to help her mother and Ichabod, but before she reached the kitchen door, the two of them made their way out with the evening meal, each of them balancing several serving plates and bowls.

"Ichabod, dear, please put those on the table while I speak with Katrina," Regina said, continuing once he was down the hallway and out of earshot, "Your

Mr. Crane is a very fine fellow, taking your father and Brom in stride like that and holding his own. I like this young man very much." She smiled at her daughter and added, "There are a couple more things on the counter we couldn't manage, dear; will you please grab them and bring them into the dining room?"

"Of course, Mama. Papa and Brom are still outside smoking. And he isn't my Mr. Crane. *Not yet.*" Her mother sighed. Katrina was happy her mother approved of Ichabod. She was worried she would hold the kiss against him, but it seemed she had completely forgotten about it, and all of her wrath was directed at Brom and her father.

"I'll let them know dinner is almost on the table, but not before you've had a moment to chat with your Mr. Crane," she said with a wink. Katrina couldn't believe her mother was being so cheeky and so open-minded about Ichabod. Or maybe it was because she was angry with her father for bringing Brom home for dinner and this was her mom's way of needling him. She didn't know, but she hadn't expected this. She had expected her mother to rail against Mr. Crane for fear she would throw over Brom, but then again, she and Brom weren't officially engaged. It was always just assumed they would marry, and Katrina thought that was one of the things that annoyed her most, everyone's assumption she would marry him without a concern for what she wanted. It felt like a done deal, and Brom thought he didn't have to try anymore. It was so refreshing to have the attentions of Mr. Crane, who seemed to be actively trying to win her favors.

Well . . . she thought, *this should be an interesting dinner party,* before she walked into the dining room.

NINE

THE GHOST IN THE COFFEE SHOP

Kat and Isadora took a break from reading, their table now covered in coffee cups, and the two of them sitting closely together on the antique velvet couch, under the approving gaze of Belle and her Beast, who seemed to be looking at them from above the fireplace. They had been reading for quite some time, only to take small breaks to get more coffee from the grumpy Raven, who seemed more put out the longer the girls were there.

"She can't be mad that we're taking up space; it's not like there's anyone else here," said Isadora, smirking.

"Totally—all those tips in her bat cookie jar are from us." Kat tried not to laugh; she didn't want to hurt Raven's feelings, even if she was scowling at them from across the room.

"Well, we know why she's really mad. She likes you, and she's disappointed you're here with me."

Kat shook her head. "That doesn't make any sense. She's always been really weird around me."

Isadora looked like a sphinx, the keeper of secrets and wisdom, as she finished off the last of her latest cup. "That's why I think she likes you, silly. Speaking of people who act weird, you know, Crane doesn't seem too terrible to me. And I was surprised Katrina's mom likes him so much."

"But doesn't he seem really full of himself? Like he's better than everyone else?"

"Maybe that's just how Crane acts when he's nervous. Baltus and Brom were being complete jerks," said Isadora.

"That's true. Brom is the worst. I suppose between the two I'd pick Ichabod as well."

"Gross! Everyone knows Brom was the best choice of the two." Kat and Isadora looked up and saw Blake and some woman standing behind him. Kat had eyestrain from reading, so she couldn't make out who the woman was, but she could tell the woman didn't look happy. She looked blurry, like an old photograph that was out of focus. Kat blinked a couple of times trying to clear her vision, and the woman was gone.

"Where's that woman who was just with you?" Kat wrapped her arms around herself. She felt the same chill she had when she thought she had seen someone walk up to talk with her when Isadora was ordering their coffee earlier. This was getting to be too much, seeing this woman everywhere. Kat was starting to get concerned. It sent a horrible chill throughout her body. Maybe Blake was right and she was starting to lose her mind, forgetting things, seeing this woman last night and now today. This wasn't like her.

"What woman?" He spun around, panicked and confused, but regained his composure almost as quickly as he lost it. Blake rarely lost his cool, so it surprised Kat. "For someone who doesn't believe in ghosts, you sure do seem to be spooked by them, Kat," Blake said.

"You're one to talk, running out of the cemetery last night, away from *a horse*! What would you have done if it were actually a ghost?" Kat felt bad saying that in front of Isadora because the horse had spooked her, too. But she couldn't help it, she was still angry with Blake, although it didn't seem to faze Isadora one bit.

"Yeah, I thought the Sleepy Hollow Boys were brave ghost hunters," said Isadora, laughing, but then she stopped abruptly to ask, "Dude, what happened to your face?" Kat hadn't noticed that Blake's face was scratched and bruised, like he had gotten into a fight or something.

"Shut up, Crow, no one was talking to you!"

Kat just shook her head. He was being as childish with Isadora as Brom had been with Ichabod, and she thought it was ridiculous.

"You obviously didn't hear what happened last night," he said to Kat. "You haven't even asked if I'm okay. I mean, look at my face."

Kat hated when he got this way, but honestly, he was this way all the time lately and she had reached her limit—especially after last night. She was done; she just didn't know how to tell him. Instead, she asked, "What happened to your face?"

He just shrugged. "Like I'm going to tell you in front of Crow. What are you two doing anyway looking so cozy?" She realized he wasn't going to tell her what happened while Isadora was there, and there was no sense in asking again. In the past, she would have, but she didn't have the energy to deal with him anymore. She was tired. There was a time when something like this would derail her from being angry with him and her focus would shift to making sure he was okay, and she almost felt guilty she was so over these sorts of the-atrics she didn't even care what happened. He was alive and being his jerk self. He was okay.

"We were reading Katrina's diary." She moved away from Isadora, suddenly feeling uncomfortable and a lit-tle guilty.

"Why would you do that?" he asked disdainfully. "Why would you want to read some old diary? Seems boring." He seemed a bit nervous, which surprised Kat; he always acted as though nothing ever fazed him, unless of course he was angry with Kat, but even then he usu-ally kept an even temper. It was something about him she hated, actually. She sometimes called him a Vulcan or Mr. Spock, because he rarely if ever showed his emo-tions. It was like a badge of honor with him, something he was proud of. When they were younger, she admired that he was always calm no matter what was happen-ing, but now it felt like he lorded it over her, like he was superior and she was the emotional mess. He acted like he was the strong man who had to hold it together for the both of them, when most of the time she was react-ing to something he had done to cause her to become emotional. So, these days she found herself not sharing how she felt with him, not telling him when he hurt her feelings, or when she was sad or worried about her future in Sleepy Hollow, for fear of how he would react. It was lonely, but it was better than him belittling her for simply reacting to how he was treating her.

"Hey, Crow, can I talk with my girlfriend alone for a minute?" Kat looked up at him and found herself thinking, *I won't be your girlfriend for long.*

"Blake, don't be rude. I'm here with Isadora; you can't just send her away." She didn't want Isadora to go, and she didn't think this was the place to break up with Blake.

"No, it's cool. I have to be getting back home anyway." Isadora gathered her things into her bag and picked up the empty coffee cups.

"Are you sure?" Kat wasn't ready to say good-bye.

"Totally. Text me later," she said with a sad smile as she made her way to the counter, dropping off the empty cups with Raven.

"So are you and Crow, like, friends now?" asked Blake sitting down next to Kat.

"We are. At least I think so," she said, seeing his face more clearly now that he was sitting next to her on the couch. "What happened to your face? Did you get into a fight with someone?"

"No, I didn't get into a fight with someone. That horse chased me down, Kat, and there was someone riding it. They ran me off the path and I fell into a ravine. I thought they were going to kill me."

"Are you sure you just didn't fall when you were running?" Kat was pretty certain he was lying, but then she remembered thinking she had seen someone on the horse, too, a blond woman.

"No, Kat, I saw them. It completely freaked me out." Kat could usually tell when Blake was lying, but this time she didn't know what to think. "You realize what this means, Kat. The Headless Horseman is real. He's really real. He tried to kill me."

Kat moved away from him. "You're lying," she said, which made him flinch. He looked uncomfortable, eyeing her diary strangely, almost like he was afraid of it.

"Why don't you believe me?"

"Honestly, because you're always lying, Blake. I think you're just trying to trick me into not being angry with you for how you treated me last night."

"This is all because of that witch Crow, isn't it? What has she been saying about me?"

"This has nothing to do with Isadora. Why don't

you like her anyway?" she asked, putting the diary back
in her bag. Blake was still eyeing it.

"She's a freak. She's always talking about weird stuff
in class, like all these old references and movies. No one
but the teachers know what she's talking about." That
made Kat laugh.

"So she's like me," she said, looking him straight
in the eye.

"Kinda, yeah, and she's always acting like she's
better than everyone, showing off to the teachers." He
was staring at her bag as he talked, almost like he was
watching to see if the diary would jump out on its own.

"What's wrong, Blake? You've been looking at my
bag ever since I put Katrina's diary in there."

He looked at her like she had gone mad. "What are
you talking about? I don't care about Katrina's diary."

"Whatever." She put her bag on her lap. She wanted
something between them; she had this strange feeling
she needed something to protect her. She felt trapped
there talking to him. She wanted to go home.

"I'm the one who should be upset about last night,"
he continued. "You made me look really stupid in front
of my friends."

Kat scoffed. "I made *you* look stupid? You tried to make me think I agreed to help you and your stupid friends summon Katrina when you know I would never do something like that."

"I was mad, Kat. You're always doing stuff like this, canceling on me, forgetting when we've made plans, and now you're acting like you don't even care that I was attacked by the Headless Horseman. It makes me feel like you don't want to be with me anymore."

"I don't think I do."

She couldn't believe she'd said it aloud. She had been feeling like they should break up for a long time, but she didn't have the nerve to face it.

"Why?" He actually looked hurt and confused, maybe even on the verge of tears. She had only seen him cry once before, when she had tried to break up with him in the past, but he had talked her out of it. She wasn't going to let him do that this time. She wasn't going to listen to him say she was the one who didn't know how to be happy, how everything was her fault. And she wasn't going to believe he was going to change this time, because he always said he would, and he never did. This time she was truly done. She had had enough.

She wanted to say it was because most of the time

he ignored her. He made her feel stupid and small. He made her doubt herself and question her sanity. She wanted to tell him about all the times she had caught him in a lie, but didn't bother saying anything because she knew he would just deny it. Instead, she focused on something she knew he couldn't deny. Something he couldn't twist or use against her.

"We don't have anything in common, and we never do the things I like anymore." It sounded feeble to her the moment it came out of her mouth, but that was part of the problem as well.

"We spent our childhoods doing the stuff you liked, Kat."

"I thought you liked doing that stuff, too."

"I did; then I grew up."

"You know what, I don't even want to talk with you. Go hang out with the Sleepy Hollow Boys because we all know *they* aren't childish." She grabbed her bag, stormed passed Raven, and slammed the door behind her. The brass bell rang so loudly she was sure she had just awoken all of Sleepy Hollow's ghosts.

TEN

THE DIARY OF KATRINA VAN TASSEL

THE LEGEND OF SLEEPY HOLLOW

After that fateful dinner with my family, Brom, and Mr. Crane, the party moved into the solarium, which served as our sitting room. We made ourselves comfortable in armchairs around the grand stone fireplace, which took up the majority of the only wall in the room that wasn't comprised entirely of panes of glass.

Outside, I could see the shadows of the craggy trees in the oak grove. There was a crisp new chill in the air that meant All Hallows' Eve was approaching, and my imagination sparked with images of ghosts fluttering among the oak trees.

⌣

Katrina's mother brought in some hot chocolate with brandy and pumpkin tarts for their dessert, and for the first time that evening, Katrina was feeling completely at ease sitting in the dim light, watching the fire flicker and spark. She imagined more nights like this with Ichabod. She couldn't wait to see the entire estate alight with jack-o'-lanterns. She daydreamed about dancing with him at the Harvest Ball, and later kissing him under the star-speckled night sky.

"What are you thinking about, Katrina?" asked Crane, who was boldly sitting next to her on the love seat, leaving Brom to sulk in the wooden rocking chair right by the fireplace across from them. He was rocking in a succession of short violent bursts that told Katrina he was seething. Dinner had gone as she expected. Her father and Brom teased Ichabod, and he deflected their jabs like a champion swordsman, or rather wordsmith, running circles around the two of them, amusing both Katrina and her mother.

"I was thinking of our Autumn Harvest Ball on All Hallows' Eve," she said dreamily, imagining dancing with Crane in the oak grove among the twinkling firelights.

"Katrina, you'd better decide whom you would like

to dress as this year before we run out of time for me to make your costume," said Katrina's mother. She and Baltus were in their favorite spots, also facing the hearth, where Regina had placed the pot of hot chocolate to keep warm next to the fire.

"Ah. Is it a fancy dress ball, then?" Crane asked, trying to keep his gaze directed on Regina, for every time he made direct eye contact with Katrina, Baltus shot him a cold, steely gaze.

"Yes, it's one of our favorite traditions," said Regina, pouring more hot chocolate into Baltus's cup. "It's the most anticipated event of the year, even if I do say so myself."

"It's not fancy dress, you prat!" Brom said so loudly it gave Baltus a start, making him spit out his hot chocolate. Regina rolled her eyes at Brom as she handed her husband a napkin, slightly chuckling to herself and taking her seat again.

"It certainly sounds like a fancy dress ball to me," said Crane with a confused look on his face.

"Well, I won't be wearing a fancy dress! What do you take me for, a lady? We dress in costumes—ghosts, ghouls, werewolves, and witches. We dress as almost anything, except of course for the Headless Horseman.

But it's not *fancy dress!*" His tone was mocking. This was exactly the sort of thing that annoyed Katrina most about Brom, talking as if he was the authority on a subject when, in fact, he knew very little.

"That's what Ichabod meant, you git. That's what fancy dress means, to dress *in costume*," Katrina said, shaking her head. In all of Brom's attempts to make Ichabod feel stupid or out of place that evening, he only succeeded in making himself look foolish and ignorant. With every word, Brom sparked Katrina's interest in Ichabod more brightly. Sure, Brom was a strong, handsome man—most any woman in Sleepy Hollow would be happy to have him as a husband and raise his brood of squealing children. He was the Sleepy Hollow ideal, a hardworking and devoted man, just like her father. Almost *too* like her father. But her father loved and respected her mother. He didn't take her for granted, and it seemed they shared common ground and interests. Her father never talked down to her mother or belittled her passions, and though some of her father's ideals were old-fashioned, that was to be expected from someone of his generation. Brom, on the other hand, had no excuse other than a lack of imagination.

"Besides, Brom, anyone can wear a dress; they're not

just for ladies. Don't be such a dolt all the time." She and Brom had been drifting apart for some time, but their differences and how little they had in common were even more apparent while in Mr. Crane's company.

"That's true, Brom. Dressing outside one's gender goes back much longer than most realize. Take Mary Read, the great pirate, for example. She dressed as a man," Crane said, quickly switching his gaze from Brom to Katrina. Katrina was impressed he knew about Mary Read. She was obsessed with lady pirates and didn't have anyone to talk with about them, until that evening.

"Oh! I read about her," Katrina said. "She is so interesting! Did you know she sometimes went by Mark Read, and it was rumored she sailed very near here? Some think she buried some of her treasure in Sleepy Hollow Hills, but I doubt that's true. Why would a pirate bury their treasure where anyone could find it?" Katrina loved that Ichabod seemed truly interested in what she was talking about. "Oh! I have a splendid idea. Maybe I will dress as her for the ball!" she said excitedly. She was so happy there was someone to share these things with, someone who actually listened. And just as Ichabod was about to reply, Baltus cleared his throat.

Everyone looked in his direction. He didn't look

pleased. Katrina didn't know if it was because they were talking about notorious pirates or if it was because his plan to have Brom to dinner only succeeded in making Crane look more appealing. Whatever was on Baltus's mind, it made him rather grumpy. He took the last sip of his hot chocolate and made a big show of yawning. Katrina knew what that meant. It was time to say goodbye to Mr. Crane.

"It's getting rather late; perhaps I should have a carriage take Mr. Crow back to town. I wouldn't want him getting frightened by the Headless Horseman alone on Sleepy Hollow Road," said Baltus with a wink to Brom. Katrina winced. She had hoped her father and Brom would have given up their relentless teasing of Mr. Crane.

"Oh, Baltus, hush," Regina chided. But both of the men seemed to delight as Crane's eyes grew wide with wonder, and perhaps even fright. Though Regina remained calm and polite on the surface, Katrina could tell she was being pushed to her limits, and she knew by the look on her mother's face that her father was in for an earful later. And Brom was surely going to hear about his behavior the next time she saw him.

"I've been meaning to ask, who exactly is this Headless Horseman everyone has been talking about?

I assume he is some sort of apparition, since Brom mentioned him in that context, but I wonder, why is it that no one dresses like him for the Harvest Ball?" Crane asked.

Brom and Baltus erupted in laughter.

"It's just not done, sir! To dress like the Headless Horseman would be an insult to his memory." Baltus gave Crane a disapproving look, which made Katrina scoff.

"According to legend, dressing like the spectral Hessian evokes his spirit, and he will surely take his revenge on anyone who dares to take on his guise," said Brom, leaning back in his chair, clearly happy to take the upper hand with Crane once more. Kat could see he was truly in his element, spinning ghost tales with Baltus and needling Crane, and she didn't like it one bit.

"But who exactly is this dreaded fellow?" Crane leaned forward like he was waiting for a fantastic tale and wanted to listen closely.

"The better question is, who *was* this dreaded fellow? Since he's *dead*!" Brom's voice was booming and dramatic, mercilessly mocking Crane. The look on his face showed that he thought he had at last outsmarted this man who had swept into Sleepy Hollow with the sole purpose of spiriting his Katrina away, but Crane didn't lose a beat.

"Well, I surmised as much, good sir, since he is no longer in possession of his head, and I did after all refer to him as an apparition, but perhaps I should have used the word *ghost* so that you could better grasp the meaning," said Crane, making Regina and Katrina laugh. Crane was too clever for Brom's insipid tomfoolery, and she was happy her mother seemed to be making the same observation.

"The Headless Horseman is no laughing matter, Mr. Crow!" Brom said, looking around the room theatrically, as if he was afraid the Headless Horseman was lurking in a corner listening to them from the shadows. Katrina could see this talk was actually making Ichabod nervous, for he was now scanning every dark corner for the headless ghost. She was surprised a man of his intellect would be so superstitious, but then again, he was hearing these tales for the first time.

"That's right, young man," Baltus joined in. "You'd do well to keep your wits about you, because the Headless Horseman can appear at any time—*especially* on the road that connects the churchyard to the battlefield, for that is where it is believed he lost his head due to an unfortunate collision with the stray cannonball. Though he has been seen by the residents of our town in the most surprising places and when they least expect it."

Crane grabbed Katrina's hand out of fright without even thinking, and it made her nervous that her father might see.

"Oh, stop it, the both of you! You're going to frighten poor Ichabod," said Katrina, quickly releasing Crane's hand before her father noticed.

"I assure you I am not the least bit frightened, Miss Katrina. I don't for one moment believe this Spectral Rider is real. It's all poppycock and folderol," said Crane, but Katrina could tell he was truly spooked.

"It's true, I tell you! And should you ever encounter the dreaded beast on Sleepy Hollow Road, make haste to the covered bridge, because once across you will be safe." Brom motioned with his arms, casting ominous shadows on the walls that made Ichabod flinch. It sent the two great bulls into fits of laughter again.

"And to what aim does this grotesquerie ride around Sleepy Hollow, can you tell me that, sirs?"

Brom and Baltus couldn't be more delighted that they were succeeding in getting Crane so worked up.

"He's searching for his head, of course," said Baltus.

"And what would this Headless Horseman do should I or anyone else ever cross his path?" Crane played it off as if he wasn't actually nervous, but Katrina could feel his leg bouncing with nervousness next to hers.

"He'd chop your head right off!" said Brom, making a wild slashing motion with his hand. Crane laughed nervously and glanced at the clock.

Baltus and Brom seemed to be enjoying themselves for the first time that evening, as Mr. Crane shifted uncomfortably in his seat. "You do well to check the time, young Crow, because it is said the Spectral Rider is most powerful at the Witching Hour, and it is quickly approaching," said Baltus, his voice low and menacing but his eyes twinkling with glee.

Then suddenly there was a loud crash against one of the windows. Everyone jumped, and poor Crane looked as though he had come completely out of his skin.

"What in heaven's name was that?" asked Regina, standing up to see what might have happened.

"Stay there, Regina. Brom and I will go see," said Baltus. "Unless you want to come with us to help investigate, Mr. Crow," he added with a sly smirk.

"I'll stay here and protect the ladies," Crane said nervously. His eyes shifted apprehensively around the room. Katrina was livid with her father and Brom for turning a perfectly delightful evening into chaos with their shameless bullying.

Baltus and Brom were laughing heartily as they went out one of the sets of French doors and disappeared into the darkness. "What is it, Baltus? What's out there?" Regina asked, taking her shawl from the back of her chair and wrapping it around her tightly against the chill coming in from the open French doors.

"It's just an owl, Regina. He must have smacked into the window, the poor thing," Baltus said as he came back inside, followed closely by Brom. Katrina felt like both Brom and her father were having too much fun at Mr. Crane's expense, but she worried if she flew to his defense too often neither of them would be any closer to respecting him.

"It's an ill omen, a bird dying on your threshold," said Brom. "And on your first visit to this house, Crow. I don't think that bodes well for you."

"Balderdash!" said Crane, his voice cracking as he quickly got up from his seat and fidgeted nervously. "And my name is *Crane*!" he added, clearly in a state of agitation. "Mr. Ichabod *Crane*!"

Katrina felt dreadful for Mr. Crane. Brom and her

father had thoroughly spooked him. It had all gotten out of hand before she realized Mr. Crane was actually frightened, but how could he not be? He wasn't raised in Sleepy Hollow and didn't grow up with tales of ghosts around the fire. This was the first time he was hearing these stories, so it was no wonder the poor fellow was frightened out of his wits. She decided she needed to do something to help him save face.

"Nonsense, everyone. Mr. Crane is a respected schoolteacher and isn't susceptible to your silly superstitions," Katrina said, standing up to join him.

"Certainly not!" said Crane, peering out the window nervously, no doubt on the lookout for the Headless Horseman. "It's suddenly occurred to me that it's quite late, and I have a very busy workday tomorrow," he added, his voice wobbling with apparent nerves.

This sent Brom and Baltus off, laughing at him again.

"How straining could *your* work be?" asked Brom.

"That's enough," Regina said sternly, giving Brom and Baltus reproving looks. Katrina was happy her mother stepped in. "Mr. Crane is right. It is quite late, and I believe it's time to end the evening. Brom, would you be so kind as to wake the stable boy and ask him to bring a carriage around for Mr. Crane when you go to saddle up Washington?" Regina looked annoyed with both her husband and Brom.

"I walked here, Miss Regina, and I'm not afraid of encountering sprits on my way home," Brom said. "But I'll be happy to wake the stable boy. Poor Mr. Crow here, bless his heart, should take a carriage home. He looks paler than a ghost!" Brom let out a vicious laugh.

Crane looked from Baltus to Brom to Regina, and then finally his gaze landed on Katrina, who was watching him carefully. She hated seeing him so nervous. He swallowed hard with an audible gulp, his Adam's apple bobbing, and said, "That won't be necessary, Mrs. Van Tassel. I assure you, I will be quite fine to walk home and fit to tell the tale the next time we see each other." Crane put on a brave face, but Katrina wasn't convinced. She didn't want him walking home alone on Sleepy Hollow Road, not after being teased so mercilessly by her father and Brom.

"I think you should take the carriage, Ichabod. No one walks Sleepy Hollow Road during the Witching Hour, not even Brom; he's just showing off." Katrina took him by the arm. "Come along, I'll show you where we hung up your coat and hat," she said, glaring at Brom and her father.

Once they got to the vestibule, Katrina turned abruptly to Crane, startling him. "There is no need to put on a show for me, Ichabod. Brom is a fool, and jealous because he knows I fancy you," she said, then caught herself and stopped before she said more. "I'm sorry, Mr. Crane; I'm mortified. I should have never said that. It's just . . ." She felt her cheeks burn red with embarrassment, but Crane cut her off.

"No need to say more, my dear Katrina. I am similarly smitten, and I am relieved to hear you feel the same. And please, for the last time, call me Ichabod," he said, kissing her hand and looking into her eyes. Katrina hadn't noticed how striking Ichabod's eyes were—catlike, dark brown with unusually long, thick lashes. Just then Regina came into the room, and the two broke apart.

"It was so delightful having you to dinner, Mr. Crane, but I'm afraid we never discussed the particulars in having you tutor our Katrina," she said, adding with a bit of cheek, "though I imagine you won't mind coming by again, say, this Monday, after your class lets out, before Baltus gets home?"

Crane's eyes widened. "That would be most agree-able, Mrs. Van Tassel," he said with a goofy grin that made Katrina's heart smile. She was completely dis-armed by this man. Though he could speak with authority on almost any subject and seemed to possess the greatest self-confidence, she loved that there was a harmlessly eccentric yet charming quality about him.

"Please call me Regina," her mother said, her eyes gleaming with approval.

"Thank you, Miss Regina," said Crane with a chaste kiss for her hand, making Katrina's mother blush. Katrina was almost sure she had never seen her mother blush before, but Mr. Crane, for all of his goofiness, did have a way of bewitching the ladies.

⌐

The air had a bone-chilling quality as they all stood on the front porch of the Van Tassel home, saying their good-byes to Brom and Ichabod. The oak grove was particularly dark that night with the moon hiding behind dark clouds, and Katrina felt a surge of panic spread though her as she imagined Ichabod making his way through the dark grove, and then along Sleepy Hollow Road alone.

"Good night, my boy!" Baltus called out to Brom, who was already making his way through the grove. Brom turned around and waved, with a wide grin on his face.

"Good night, Baltus! See you bright and early tomorrow!" He walked backward as he waved and added, "And good night, my dear Katrina and Miss Regina." He blew Katrina a kiss, which made her and her mother cringe.

Ichabod was still standing on the dirt path that led to the oak grove, shuffling his feet and fidgeting nervously. "Farewell, Van Tassels. You are fine and gracious hosts. I am truly honored to have been invited into your lovely home. Katrina, my fond memories of this evening shall sustain me until I have the good fortune of being in your exquisite company once again," he said before starting down the path that would take him to Sleepy Hollow Road.

"Good night, Ichabod. I, too, look forward to seeing you again." Katrina didn't dare say more with her father standing there. She wanted to run to Ichabod and implore him to take the carriage. And in an even more secret place in her heart, she wanted to kiss him. A deep and penetrating fear was mounting within her, as she saw poor Ichabod looking over his shoulder, hesitating before he set off into the dark oak grove. The Van Tassels shivered on the porch as Crane slowly made his way down the path, trailing behind Brom, who was about twenty feet or so ahead of him. And just as they were about to turn around and head back inside the house, they heard Brom's voice booming in the distance.

"BEWARE OF THE HEADLESS HORSEMAN!" he bellowed, and Katrina could hear Brom laughing as he disappeared into the darkness.

"We can get you a carriage, Ichabod," Katrina shouted.

But Baltus answered for him. "You don't need a carriage, do you, Crow? Not a strapping young lad such as yourself." Baltus gave Katrina the side-eye. "Just make sure to stay to the path, and if you hear the clatter of horse hooves behind you, run like the wind to the covered bridge!"

Poor Mr. Crane looked terrified. Then Baltus took Katrina and Regina by the arms to lead them back inside. "Come on, my dears, it's much too cold and late. Mr. Crow will be just fine," he said, with an impish twinkle in his eye, making both Katrina and Regina glare at him.

"Katrina, you go inside, I want to have words with your father," said Regina, giving Baltus a seething look, and Katrina felt happy to have her mother on her side.

⌣

As Brom made his way down Sleepy Hollow Road, he was feeling rather chuffed. "Crane is intolerable! There is no way Katrina will choose him over me!" he said to no one as he made his way home.

Sleepy Hollow Road was flanked by a canopy of oak trees that almost obscured the night sky. Brom wished he had asked for a lantern to light his way, but he didn't want to appear weak or frightened, though he was soon thankful he came to a stretch that was illumined by moonlight. He thought Katrina would find it beautiful walking this path, with the moonlight peeking through the branches. He missed their walks in the woods, talking about the books she read and all the places she wanted to travel, but when they were young, he thought it was just that. Dreams. He didn't realize when Katrina got older she would want to leave Sleepy Hollow, and want to leave him. He wouldn't admit it, but he was hurt by her desire to leave, hurt that she stopped sharing her thoughts and feelings with him. Ever since he had to go to work for Baltus on the farm, he felt closed off from her, but he didn't have the words to tell her how he had been feeling. He didn't have the time to read as he once did; he had to work and therefore had nothing exciting to share with her at the end of his day. But he kept that to himself, and let his resentment fester. He didn't know how to make things better with her. He felt trapped in their new patterns, circling upon them over and over, hoping to reach the center again—for that is what Katrina was for him, his center, his heart, and if they could just find their way back, things would be as they were. But he felt like he was lost in a labyrinth, trying to find her, and he was starting to realize it was perhaps himself he was searching for.

As he walked down Sleepy Hollow Road, he felt a strange chill that penetrated his very core, making his bones ache and his heart race. He looked through the canopy of oak trees that swayed in the breeze, revealing dark, ominous clouds. He buttoned up his coat, turning up his collar against the cold wind, and walked faster, suddenly feeling nervous. He felt as if someone was following him. He felt foolish but couldn't help but look behind him, and gasped when he saw glowing eyes in the hollow of a tree.

"It's only an owl, you dolt!" he said aloud. "You're acting like poor Mr. Crow." He laughed to himself, wondering how Ichabod was faring on his journey.

"That coward is probably up a tree like a scared cat!" he said, howling with laughter so loud it frightened the owl, which took flight. He watched as the owl flew through a clearing in the branches, glowing white from the light of the moon.

The wind picked up, causing tree branches and dry leaves to fall and stir along the path, and with each step, he heard a crunch under his feet. Strangely, it sounded as if there was another pair of feet following behind him, and the crunching noise sounded like breaking bones. *Crunch crunch crunch.* He quickly turned around and saw no one there, but every time he took a step, he heard another step behind him and the sickening sound of bones crunching underfoot. He quickened his pace, the leaves stirring on the path swirling around him and kicking dust into his eyes. As he was rubbing his eyes, he heard the chime of the Sleepy Hollow clock tower, which sent a terrible lurching feeling in his stomach. The bell rang twelve times.

Midnight. The Witching Hour. He stood on the path for a few moments after the last ring, listening carefully to see if he could hear anyone else coming along the path, and then he heard it, the deafening sound of horse hooves galloping toward him. He was panicked, but saw he was near the Oldest Tree and decided it was a safe place to hide. He ran over to the giant oak and hid within the hollow as best as he could. As he crouched there trembling from the cold and fright, he could hear the beating of his heart pounding faster and faster, matching the relentless sound of hooves slamming on the path coming toward him. He didn't dare look out from the hollow of the tree for fear the horseman would see him. The heartbeat sound was deafening, and he realized it wasn't only his own heartbeat he was hearing; another heartbeat was coming from inside the tree, pulsing with each thud. He recoiled, horrified, and when he stepped back, he noticed there was something glistening in the moonlight on the forest floor. It looked almost black, and thick, and when he reached down to touch it, it felt warm and sticky on his fingers. He moved into a shard of moonlight streaming down though the branches so he could see what the warm thick liquid was, and to his horror, he realized it was blood. It was pouring out of the hollow of the Oldest Tree, pooling at his feet. He staggered back, horrified, knocking into a low-hanging branch that snagged on his coat.

"Great Hollow's Ghost!" he screamed, thinking someone or something had him by the collar, for indeed the branch looked like skeletal claws, and he could swear the tree was alive, enchanted by some unnamed ghost or demon who haunted the path. He screamed in bloody terror, twisting and turning, trying to free himself from the tree branch, and then he saw the spectral demon himself: the Headless Horseman.

He was more horrifying than Brom had ever imagined. What terrified him most was how real this demon appeared, astride his beast of a horse. He looked as the legend said, wearing his Hessian uniform and long black cloak that billowed behind him as he charged toward him. Brom's heart was pounding so violently within his chest, he was sure he was going to die of a heart attack before the headless Hessian trooper even reached him. Finally, Brom was able to free himself from the branches, ripping his coat, and falling forward into the pool of blood. He lay on his stomach looking up to see a black horse rearing up, and then slamming its hooves into the ground only inches from his face. Brom rolled to the side, off the path, scrambled to his feet, and ran as fast as he could, not daring to stop to look behind, running and running, with the relentless clatter of hooves behind him. It wasn't until he was home that he realized the Headless Horseman had abandoned his pursuit.

ELEVEN

THE REQUITED HEART

Kat closed Katrina's diary, and took a deep breath. Again, she felt as if she were in the wrong place or the wrong time after she stopped reading and realized she was back home in her room. Katrina's diary had such vivid descriptions, Kat felt as if she was transported, and she was experiencing everything as if it were happening to her. Her heart was racing, and she had to tell Isadora about what she had read.

Kat
5:17
OMG! I think Headless Horseman might be real

Isadora
5:18
What?! Really? What happened?

Kat
5:19
Something I read in Katrina's diary. Want
to meet at the Oldest Tree tomorrow? I can
just show you, it's kinda freaking me out

Isadora
5:20
Totally! What time?

Kat
5:21
Noon?

Isadora
5:22
Perfect! See you then! ♥

Kat was surprised that Isadora included a heart at
the end of her text. It made her feel giddy and nervous
all at once. She wondered if she should send one back or
not, and she sat there overthinking it, wondering why
she was hesitating. She had been thinking about how
Isadora stood up to Blake and his friends, and how for
the first time in a while she felt completely comfortable
with someone, and reasoned a heart emoji wasn't out of
order. *You're being silly*, she thought. *She sent the heart first.*
So, she took a deep breath and pressed send.

Kat
5:27
YAY! See you then! ♥

Kat sat there for a moment just looking at her phone. Her stomach was full of bats, which was something people in Sleepy Hollow said rather than butterflies. She wondered if she should have sent the heart after all. Maybe Isadora didn't even notice, but she kept looking at her phone hoping Isadora would reply, and she wasn't even sure what she wanted her to say. But then her phone dinged, and Isadora's reply made her heart happy.

Isadora
5:31
♥ !!!

Kat smiled. It had been so long since someone made her so happy with a single text message. It wasn't since she and Blake were young together that she'd enjoyed someone's company so much. Kat's stomach was in knots. Everything in her world was shifting, but for the first time, she was starting to feel like she could direct her own life. She felt as if she was allowing herself to see Blake clearly, and not just because seeing him through Isadora's eyes at the cemetery that night was so surreal. She didn't even feel like herself when it was all happening. She felt like she was looking at herself from a distance, wondering who she was and how she had let things with Blake get to this point. But it had been a gradual thing, happening slowly over time. They had been together for so long, and she supposed she had become used to her unhappiness. It had become familiar. Blake would say she preferred to be unhappy, but she was starting to feel while reading Katrina's diary that she was slowly waking from a horrible dream, and she realized this was not the way she wanted to spend the rest of her life.

It was unnerving to read Katrina's story and see the similarities in her own life. Both of them were being pressured by their families to marry someone they weren't sure they loved, and it took both of them a long time to find the courage to break things off with men who treated them poorly. She *had* tried breaking things off with Blake in the past, so many times, but he always found a way to make her think it was her fault, like she was the one who was incapable of being happy. Like there was something wrong with her. She realized today, maybe for the first time, there was something wrong with Blake, and not her. She knew if something were to come of her friendship with Isadora, Blake would feel like she had broken up with him for her, but that wasn't true. She sat there thinking about everything she had read in Katrina's diary and wondered how it was possible she and Katrina had so much in common. They both grew up to be with their childhood sweethearts only to find they had outgrown them, and both of their heads were turned by someone who wasn't from Sleepy Hollow. Suddenly Kat was even more excited and nervous to read the rest of Katrina's diary to see how things really went down with Ichabod. Of course she knew the story everyone told on All Hallows' Eve, but she was eager to read Katrina's side of things for the first time.

And she was more eager than ever to see Isadora the next day, because it wasn't just the diary that had opened her eyes.

⌣

The next morning, Kat went down to the kitchen to get herself a cup of coffee. She hadn't realized Maddie was in the walk-in pantry, and when she came out, Kat was startled, spilling her coffee all over the counter and floor.

"You're jumpy this morning. Did you think I was a ghost?" Maddie said with her usual impish grin, and helped Kat clean up the spilled coffee.

"Sorry, Maddie. Oh, hey, did you have a good night with your gentleman friend?" Kat remembered her mother telling her she had spent the Longest Twilight with a date, and wondered what sort of guy he was. Maddie had been a fixture in their household for as long as Kat could remember. She was an older woman, with entirely silver hair and bright sparkling eyes that looked as if they were always smiling unless she was annoyed. Kat liked the idea of Maddie having someone special. She was widowed early in her marriage, and she thought Maddie would spend the rest of her life alone. She hated the idea of Maddie going home to an empty house every night.

"I did, as a matter of fact. It was a splendid evening." Maddie beamed as she reached to take a bag of flour out of the pantry. "But I must say the topic over dinner was almost entirely about you," she added, putting the flour on the large wooden counter where she and Kat's mother did their baking. It was that time of year again, when Maddie and Kat's mother would spend all their time baking and preparing for the Harvest Ball. Soon every available surface in the kitchen would be covered with baked goods, and still they would be afraid they hadn't baked enough. Kat wondered why anyone would spend their evening talking about her, especially on a date.

"You were talking about me? Why?"

"We all wondered why you weren't at the Longest Twilight ceremony; you are the *reigning Katrina* after all," she said with a wink. Maddie and Katrina's mother both liked to wink. It was their thing.

"If anyone is the *reigning Katrina*, it's Mom," said Kat, laughing at Maddie. She was a strange sort of woman, sometimes mysterious, and always funny. Kat loved her.

"Well, I'm just happy you made it home safe. Your mother told me what happened, of course. Out late again reading your books. I swear, you're more like the first Katrina every day. You know, she loved to read. She wanted to be a writer." Maddie got some eggs and milk from the large old-fashioned refrigerator. "I keep telling your mother to replace these relics, but she insists on keeping this old refrigerator and stove. If she had it her way, we'd still have a wood-burning stove and an icebox in here," she said, cracking an egg into a yellow bowl.

Kat thought Maddie was right. Her mother did love

to preserve the Van Tassel history in any way she could. She wondered what her mom was going to think when she told her she broke up with Blake. She wasn't ready to have that conversation with her. She didn't want to hear about how they hoped she and Blake would get married and run the estate together. She was sick of that conversation.

"I didn't know Katrina wanted to be a writer," said Kat, pouring herself a cup of coffee.

"There's a lot most people don't know about her, but I suppose that will all change now that you're reading her diary. I told your mom a long time ago to give it to you. I'm happy she finally did," she said, mixing the eggs and milk into the flour.

"I am, too, Maddie. And she's a really good writer. She writes very descriptively. I can see everything she says. It's like a little movie playing in my head when I read her diary." Kat leaned on the counter, drinking her coffee. She loved chatting with Maddie. They often did this while Maddie made her pies.

"I imagine one day you'll announce you're going off to New York to become a writer," she said, dusting the wooden table with flour.

Kat hadn't told anyone this was her plan. "What makes you think that, Maddie?" she asked, narrowing her eyes at the older woman.

"Let's just say Maddie knows things," Maddie said. Her raspy laugh sounded like rustling branches in the wind.

"What if I do decide I want to move away and become a writer? How you do think my mom would feel?" asked Kat, giving Maddie the side-eye.

"It would break her heart, of course," she said, "But you have to do what's good for you, Kat. Even though Katrina chose her own path, she regrets not following some of her dreams."

Kat narrowed her eyes at Maddie. "You talk as if she is still alive," Kat said, watching Maddie roll out the dough for the pies.

"She is still very much alive in the hearts and minds of everyone in Sleepy Hollow," Maddie said with an uncharacteristically serious look on her face.

"You don't mean she is one of the ghosts who haunt Sleepy Hollow?"

"That's exactly what I mean, Kat. I often chat with her under the Oldest Tree." She cut the pie crust with a large metal stamp in the shape of a pumpkin, as if what she had just said was the most normal thing in the world. That is how it was in Sleepy Hollow. Kat was surrounded by people who not only believed in ghosts but thought they'd spoken to them, and she was starting to wonder what she really believed herself. Especially after reading what Katrina wrote about Brom's encounter with the Headless Horseman, and now with this mysterious woman following her around.

"Maddie, you know I love you, but do you really expect me to believe you chat with Katrina's ghost? I spend a lot of time at the Oldest Tree and I've never seen her there."

Maddie's crackly laugh rang out. "I know, my dear. She often talks about your visits to her favorite tree. She loves your company."

Maddie's words sent a chill though Kat. The idea of the first Katrina haunting the Oldest Tree sent a panic though her. When Kat was young, she lived in almost constant fear of ghosts, and it wasn't until she stopped believing that her anxiety was quelled. Now that she was uncertain, she felt the panic growing within her again. That's why she needed to talk with Isadora. Even though Isadora believed in spirits, she seemed more sensible about the supernatural than most people in Sleepy Hollow. Maybe it was because she was an outsider.

Kat looked at her phone; it was almost eleven. Kat had lost track of time chatting with Maddie, and she almost forgot she was meeting Isadora at noon.

Just then Kat's mother walked into the kitchen. She wanted to talk with her, tell her how happy she was she had given her Katrina's diary, but she worried if she started discussing it she would never stop, and she didn't want to get on the topic of Blake. She'd be trapped there forever if she told her they had broken up. There were so many things running through her mind, and there was a lot of it she didn't understand, so she wanted to wait until she had it all sorted out.

"Good morning, Mom. I'm really sorry to rush off, but I have to get ready. I'm meeting a new friend in about an hour," she said, pouring herself another cup of coffee, with an apologetic smile for her mom.

"Who is this friend?" her mom asked. "I know all your friends."

"Her name is Isadora Crow. She's new in town," she said, trying to skirt her way out of the kitchen. But the look on her mom's face stopped her. She looked like she had seen, well, a ghost.

"Did you say Isadora *Crow*?" Trina put her hand to her heart and glanced at Maddie.

"I did. Why are you making those faces?"

"Nothing, dear, I just . . ." She paused and collected herself. "A newcomer to Sleepy Hollow! We don't get a lot of those and I guess I'm just wary of you spending time with someone I've never met." She still had that worried look on her face, but she was trying to hide it.

"She's really cool, Mom; I think you'll like her." Kat looked from her mom to Maddie, wondering what they weren't saying, because clearly some unspoken thing was happening between them. "What's going on with you two?" she said, furrowing her brow.

"Nothing, Kat," her mother said, fumbling with a tray of little tart tins, making them clatter. "Crow, that's an interesting name. Where does it come from?"

"You know, we didn't talk about her ancestry the first time we met," said Kat. "Seriously, what is even going on? You're both acting crazy."

"Nothing is going on. I just don't trust newcomers to this town. They're just ghost chasers and tourists, only interested in one thing. I'm not sure I'm comfortable with you spending time with her."

"*Something* is going on! You're both freaking out, and it doesn't make sense. Isadora is awesome, and I really like her, and unless you tell me what your problem is, I'm going to keep hanging out with her."

"This just feels too familiar, Kat. How far along are you in Katrina's diary?"

"What does that have to do with anything?" asked Kat, but she was sure she knew exactly what her mother meant. She just wanted to hear her mom say it; her life was starting to feel eerily similar to Katrina's. "Mom, can you and Maddie stop being weird for like one minute and calm down? She's a new friend, and I really like her. Like, a lot."

"Fine, but I want to meet this Isadora Crow. Tell her she's expected for dinner this evening."

TWELVE

THE OLDEST TREE

Kat quickly made her way down Sleepy Hollow Road. The path was covered in autumn leaves that crunched under her feet, turning into red, orange, and yellow dust. She couldn't help but remember reading about Brom walking the same path, and feeling as though he were hearing the sound of crunching bones. Every step sent a shiver through her body. Though it was known in family legend Brom had been a bit of a prankster and troublemaker, she couldn't imagine him making up a story about the Headless Horseman, let alone telling Katrina how much it had frightened him. He didn't seem like the sort of man who willingly admitted he was scared. This was but one of the ways Kat felt her world shifting. She couldn't find a logical reason for Brom being dishonest about his encounter with the

Headless Horseman, which meant maybe, just maybe, he could be real. And it made her wonder if Blake was telling the truth about what happened to him.

And then before she knew it, she was at the Oldest Tree.

As she approached, Kat saw Isadora sitting under the majestic oak, right where Kat usually sat. Isadora wasn't looking in her direction; she was taking photos of twisted branches with her cell phone. Katrina could almost see the photos in her mind; she imagined they were stark black-and-white like the old movies she loved so much. She stood there for a moment just watching Isadora take photos. She loved looking at her. She loved her long, straight black hair, her large intense eyes that sometimes seemed a little sad, and her exceedingly long and thick eyelashes. She was trying to remember the name of the old actress who had lashes like that naturally. Then she recalled that it was Elizabeth Taylor. But Isadora looked more like a silent-film actress. Her features had a ghostly quality to them, or maybe they were just old-fashioned. She didn't look like she belonged in their time period, but like a ghostly image from the past still brimming with life and personality. But what Kat loved most in that moment was watching the way

Isadora looked at the tree and contemplated the light. It was so intimate and personal, she almost felt like she shouldn't have been there, but she was so happy she was. Just then Isadora must have felt Kat standing there, because she looked up from her phone and smiled.

"I'm sorry! I wasn't trying to be creepy. I didn't want to startle or interrupt you while you were taking photos," said Kat, feeling a bit embarrassed.

"You're good. Come sit next to me, I want to show you something I found." Isadora reached out her hand. Kat wasn't sure if Isadora meant for her to take her hand, but she decided to anyway and felt her stomach flip when Isadora didn't let go after she sat down. They sat there together under the tree holding hands, and Kat couldn't have been happier.

"Oh, hey, may I see the photos you were taking?"

"Totally." Isadora handed over her phone. Blake would have never let her look through his phone. He wouldn't let it out of his sight and acted like she was jealous and possessive if she asked who he was texting. Spending time with Isadora just felt easier. Kat had never had a best girl friend, and she wasn't sure if this was how best girl friends felt about each other. She would see girls at school holding hands and being very intimate with each other, but they were just friends. This felt different, or at least she thought it did. This felt like something else entirely, and it excited and frightened her. *I really like her.*

The photos Isadora took were exactly as she imagined: stark, beautiful, and black-and-white. One of the photos reminded her of something she read in Katrina's diary. "These are so lovely, Isadora," she said, showing her the one that sparked her memory. "See here how these dark leaves look like blood?" she asked, instantly feeling weird she said that. "I mean, maybe you don't think so, but . . ."

"I know which one you're talking about; I thought the same thing," she said, smiling at Kat.

"What? Why are you smiling like that?" Kat asked.

"I just really love the way your mind works, Kat Van Tassel," she said, making Kat blush.

"I'm so happy you texted me," said Isadora, smiling. The corners of her eyes wrinkled in a way Kat found endearing. She suddenly felt herself wanting to kiss the corners of her eyes and the deep asymmetrical dimples she had on each of her cheeks, which made her feel flushed and nervous. And then she understood why her mother and Maddie were so freaked out. They knew she had feelings for Isadora. Maddie and Kat's mother didn't dabble in witchcraft, but they did seem to have some supernatural power to know what was going on with her, sometimes before she even knew it herself.

Suddenly, all she wanted to do was run away. She was afraid of her feelings, afraid of the parallel experiences she was sharing with the first Katrina, and afraid because her mother and Maddie were so concerned. But before she could make up an excuse to leave, she got caught up in Isadora's eyes flashing in the sunlight that was peeking through the canopy of branches. She wondered if she should tell Isadora about breaking up with Blake. She hadn't heard from him since she left him at the café, which surprised her. When she had tried to break things off in the past, he'd hound her until she agreed to talk to him again.

Kat was still feeling a bit nervous, but something kept her sitting there with Isadora. She liked being in her company and liked the feel of her hand in hers. She thought she had just been excited to share what she had read in Katrina's diary, but she realized she also wanted a reason to see Isadora. Then the panic struck her again. She quickly let go of Isadora's hand and stood up.

"I'm sorry. Maybe this was a bad idea," she said,

looking around as if she was afraid someone was there watching them. She had been feeling that way ever since she started seeing the blond woman, and it unnerved her.

"Oh my god, I'm so sorry. I'm making you uncomfortable. I thought maybe you were attracted to me; I guess was wrong. And it's awful of me to do this while you're with someone else. I'm so sorry," Isadora said, standing up to meet Kat's gaze and taking her by both of her hands. There it was, the real reason Kat was nervous. She hadn't known until that moment how Isadora felt about her, and now that she knew, she wasn't feeling nervous anymore. She knew exactly why she was there. She felt the same way.

"You're not wrong. And I broke up with Blake yesterday at the café after you left," Kat said, blushing and lowering her gaze again, willing herself not to kiss Isadora, because that was all she wanted to do in that moment.

"What happened? What did he do?"

Kat didn't want to talk about it; she wasn't sure she wanted Isadora to know all the reasons she had broken up with Blake, because there were so many more than what happened at the café, or even at the cemetery.

"It's okay if you don't want to talk about it."

Kat sighed with relief, but not feeling pressured just made her want to open up.

"It's just, I feel so ashamed for letting him treat me like that for so long, and not realizing how much he made me doubt myself. I'm not sure I want to tell you everything that happened, I want you to know who I am, or rather who I want to be now that I'm not with him anymore."

Isadora took Kat's face in her hands. "You have nothing to be ashamed of, Kat Van Tassel, nothing, do you hear me? He is the one who should be ashamed for how he lied and manipulated you." But then Isadora looked like she was distracted, like something was bothering her. Her eyes were full of fear and what Kat thought looked like remorse.

"What's wrong? What did I say? You really do think I'm an idiot for staying with Blake for so long, don't you? Because I honestly wouldn't blame you if you did."

Isadora shook her head. "You're not an idiot, Kat. Don't ever think that. You can tell me anything, I promise," she said, frowning.

"I'm not used to sharing how I feel. Blake would always use it against me later or find a way to make me feel like I was unstable or something. I don't know, it's hard to explain. Everything he did was so subtle and so cunning, it was hard to call him out on it. He would always find a way to make me think I was just being paranoid, hysterical, or something, all while hiding behind his twisted version of logic and stoicism."

Isadora sighed. "He was gaslighting you. I felt like that was what he was doing at the cemetery; that's why I got so upset. I'm so sorry." Isadora's eyes started to tear up and she looked as if her heart was broken.

"What's wrong? Why are you crying? What did I do?"

"You didn't do anything, Kat. Please stop thinking everything is your fault. It's something I've done, and I don't know how to fix it." Isadora broke down in tears, sobbing in the crook of Kat's neck.

"Do you want to tell me about it? You don't have to," she said, pulling back to wipe away Isadora's tears with the cuff of her sweater. "I seem to be making everyone upset today. When I told my mom and her friend Maddie I was meeting you today, they totally freaked out. She said something like my story and Katrina's were too similar. I thought she was just talking about how both Katrina and I had fallen for new people in town, but now I wonder if there is more to it than that."

Isadora put her hands on her face, rubbing above her eyes as if she had a headache, and then pushed her hair back out of her face.

"I'm sure there is; in fact I know there is," she said, but then they heard a noise that startled them. "Wait, did you hear that?" The noise sounded like leaves crunching underfoot, as if someone was trying to sneak up on them. They both stopped what they were doing, trying to be as quiet as possible.

"Shh, I think someone is there," Kat whispered, right before they heard the loud snap of a branch and someone or something scrambling quickly away. They rushed to the direction of the noise, but they didn't find anyone there. What they did find, however, was even more disturbing.

Just beyond the trees was a circle of extinguished candles surrounding a raised patch of grass. At the head of the mound was a large, smooth stone. Someone had used black powder and chalk to cover it in hastily scrawled symbols.

"What is this?" Kat kneeled down, a bad feeling creeping down her neck.

"I think it's a grave," said Isadora, kneeling next to Kat. "But there's no name."

"How have I never seen this tombstone?"

"It might have been covered. It looks like someone moved away all those leaves and branches." Isadora took out her phone and took photos. "I'm going to look up what these symbols mean. They look like summoning-spell talismans, but I'm not sure," she said, taking photos from every direction. "I wonder who is buried here, and why someone would want to summon them? I think it's weird there's no name on the stone."

"Oh, I don't know," said Kat. "I bet I know what's going on. The Sleepy Hollow Boys were probably just doing one of their stupid rituals out here. They don't even know what they're doing half the time. I'm sure it's nothing to worry about." Kat stood up, suddenly remembering the reason they met. "I think I'm just letting stuff get to me. Reading Katrina's diary really freaked me out last night."

"But did you hear the same noise I did just now? Who was there? Were they watching us?" Isadora was looking around the hollow, scanning it for anything that looked amiss.

"The candle wax is hard. I don't think anyone was just there. The noise was probably just an animal," said Kat. "Come on, you have to read about the night Brom was attacked by the Horseman. It's really creepy." She took Isadora's hand and led her back to the Oldest Tree— the very spot where Brom had his encounter with the Headless Horseman. "See right here?" she said, pointing at the hollow of the tree. "Brom told Katrina he saw blood gushing out of here right before the Headless Horseman showed up."

"So, do you think it was actually the Headless Horseman?" Isadora still looked upset or nervous, but Kat didn't know how to bring up what they had been talking about before they got distracted by whatever the Sleepy Hollow Boys had been doing in the Hollow. She didn't want to pressure her.

"I'm not sure. I mean, I can't imagine Brom would tell Katrina he was attacked by the Headless Horseman if he hadn't been. Family legend paints him as a proud man," Kat said.

The girls sat back down near the hollow of the tree, this time a little closer so they could read together. Kat was distracted by the feeling of Isadora's leg alongside her own. She wanted to look up at her again, any reason to look into her eyes, but she didn't dare. Instead, she kept her eyes down on the page, but she couldn't help but feel like Isadora was looking at her.

"I left off right before the infamous Harvest Ball, so we just need to backtrack so you can read about what happened to Brom," Kat said, still looking at the diary.

"Is the Harvest Ball the night the Headless Horseman scared Ichabod off?" asked Isadora, looking as if she felt nervous again.

"That's what local legend says, but I assumed it was actually Brom because he was jealous Katrina was so fond of him. I always wondered how Katrina felt about Ichabod just running off like that," said Kat. "I just remembered something. Baltus called Ichabod Mr. Crow instead of Mr. Crane. And your last name is Crow. I'm wondering if that's why my mom freaked out that you and I are friends. Like our friendship is reminding her of Katrina and Ichabod's. She literally insisted you come to dinner tonight so she can meet you."

Isadora's smile looked strained, like she wanted to say something but was too afraid. "What did you say to your mom about me?"

"Just that I really like you, and I think she will, too." Kat could see there was still something Isadora wanted to tell her, but she understood how hard it was for her to share things that made her vulnerable, and she didn't want to pressure Isadora if she wasn't ready yet.

But for the first time, she was feeling completely safe with someone, and she hoped Isadora would eventually feel the same and trust her with whatever had her so upset. So she decided to share something else with her, something she hadn't shared with anyone.

"I haven't told anyone this, but I really want to be an author. I've been looking at colleges in places like New York and San Francisco even though my mom doesn't want me go."

Isadora smiled. "Then you should! What's stopping you?" she asked, squeezing Kat's hand.

"I don't know. I guess my parents, their expectations, and of course there was Blake. And before I met you, there really wasn't a reason to stay."

"Don't ever let anyone stand in the way of what you want to do, Kat. Do you know where you want to go? I want to major in film and photography, and I'm sure there are schools with good programs for writing and filmmaking. Who knows, maybe we'll end up at the same college," said Isadora, making Kat's heart feel happy. The idea of them going to college together sent a thrill through her she didn't expect. This conversation would have gone completely differently if she were having it with Blake. He always dismissed the things she

felt passionately about and made her feel like she was
foolish for not wanting to stay in Sleepy Hollow, where
she had a future already laid out for her. A future that
had made her feel trapped, and would eventually drain
all the life from her. And then where would she be? In
the Van Tassel family crypt with all the other Katrinas.

"What are you thinking about?" Isadora asked.

"Nothing really, I'm just happy we met, Isadora
Crow, that's all," Kat said, smiling.

"I'm happy, too."

"So are you okay with coming to my house for dinner tonight? My mom has basically decided you're coming," said Kat, laughing.

"Well, if it's already decided, then I guess I'm coming," said Isadora nervously.

"Oh, and my mom's friend Maddie will be there.
You may feel like you're under interrogation, between
my mom, Maddie, and of course my dad, but he's sweet,"
Kat said, both of them laughing now.

"I can handle it."

"I'm sure you can," said Kat, thinking if anyone
could handle her family it was Isadora. "I think you'll
like Maddie. She's a little odd, but that's one of the reasons I love her so much. Like she told me today she sees
Katrina all the time and talks to her and stuff."

"She talks to her ghost? That's kind of rad," said Isadora, looking around as if she was a little spooked.

"Are you okay? Every time I mention the first Katrina or the Headless Horseman, you seem a bit freaked-out. Is it because of what I told you about this tree? We can read the diary at my house if you want. I don't want you to be scared."

"No, I'm okay. I always imagined ghosts to be more like imprints, like faded old photographs, impressions left over. Like I never thought of them as actual people who can think and feel and talk, but now I'm starting to wonder. Does that make sense?" asked Isadora.

"That totally makes sense. Yeah, I hate the idea of spirits walking around with all their memories of their lives, just, like, stuck here forever. There is something really sad and horrifying about it. Like the Headless Horseman: He's trapped in a nightly loop, searching for his head. That seems like a terrible existence. I remember thinking of that when I was little and first started to understand all these stories, and I felt so bad for him, and I think that's why I didn't believe he was real, because I didn't want to believe all the ghosts here were miserable. I hate to think of Katrina's ghost being trapped here, especially since she felt trapped in Sleepy Hollow when she was alive." Kat noticed that tears were forming in Isadora's eyes as she spoke. "Oh, hey, what's wrong?" she asked, wiping away one of Isadora's tears.

"You have a beautiful mind, Kat, that's all." Isadora had the saddest look on her face.

"Are you sure?" Kat asked looking into Isadora's eyes. The tears still clung to her lashes, making her eyes sparkle. It seemed like Isadora had more to say but she was too afraid. "Really, what is it?" Kat asked. Isadora looked as if she was somewhere else, spirited away by a memory.

"I guess I was just wondering if that's why you don't believe in ghosts. It didn't make sense to me at first, but I think the reason you don't believe is because you're afraid you'll be stuck in Sleepy Hollow forever."

Kat felt her stomach drop. "It terrifies me, to be honest; it's my worst nightmare. But it's more than that—the thought of ghosts surrounding us, lurking in every corner, hiding behind every tree, following us wherever we go really freaks me out. I couldn't sleep most nights when I was growing up because I was terrified of them. I haven't told anyone but Blake and my parents about this, but when I was a little girl, I was convinced a lady was haunting me. She would follow me everywhere I went. She was always with me, *always*. I saw her everywhere. And l think she might be haunting me again."

"That's crazy, who is she? What did your parents do?"

"My mom said I shouldn't be afraid, but I was always so scared. The weird thing was, when Blake and I were little, I wasn't afraid of her; she was like our friend, always there, like she was protecting us, but as we got older, he said he couldn't see her anymore, and I thought he was pretending she wasn't there, because it seemed like he did see her. I was almost sure I saw them talking at the Oldest Tree many times when he thought I wasn't looking, but he would always deny it. After a while, he said she was never there, never there at all. He said he was only pretending she was real, like it was a game we played as children that he outgrew."

Isadora narrowed her eyes. "What did she look like?"

Kat thought about it and realized she didn't remember. It was so strange, how she could not remember what *the lady* looked like. All she could remember was her blond hair.

"I honestly don't remember. It's weird because I saw her every day for so long, and now I can't even see her face in my mind. I asked Blake, but he said he didn't know because he never saw her."

"He is such a jerk. I don't think you were afraid of

ghosts, Kat. I think you were afraid you were losing your mind."

Kat was feeling the old anxious feeling she would have when she believed in ghosts, and she hated it; it was like a dark, heavy fog that usually made her feel tired and alone, but for the first time, she felt like she had someone she could talk to about it.

"It's crazy, but I think I've seen her a few times recently, at the café and at the cemetery, and honestly it's really freaking me out. What if it's the same lady?" Kat's hand was shaking.

"I know everything will be okay. You're one of the strongest women I know, Kat Van Tassel," said Isadora, making Kat smile.

"What makes you say that? We only just met. And I don't think I'm particularly strong."

"Oh, you are. You are braver than you even realize. It took a lot of courage to break up with Blake, and to open up to me after all you've been through with him. I have a feeling you're going to do great things, Kat."

Kat wanted to be all those things. She wanted to be brave and strong, but she hadn't felt that way for a very long time. She wasn't used to having a friend who was so open with their feelings. Someone who simply said what was on her mind. It had been a long time since Kat felt comfortable talking about herself and felt safe doing it. She didn't know what else to say. She wanted so badly to be the person Isadora thought she was, and she didn't want to say anything to ruin the illusion.

"Should we read Katrina's diary? Dinner is at six. I think we have some time before we have to leave."

"We have plenty of time," said Isadora, checking the time on her phone.

"Awesome. Let's get you caught up then and we can at least read everything leading up to the Harvest Ball. I skimmed some of it this morning, but I didn't want to get too far ahead before we could read it together."

"I'm so happy you want to share this with me," said Isadora.

Kat was happier in that moment than she had been in a long time, but she couldn't shake the feeling someone was watching them. So she reached inside of herself and tried to pull up that courage Isadora saw inside of her as they read Katrina's diary together. Though Kat had to wonder if someone or something was there with them reading over their shoulders.

THIRTEEN

THE DIARY OF KATRINA VAN TASSEL

THE COURTSHIP OF KATRINA VAN TASSEL

Despite the warm sun streaming through the oak branches overhead, I feel the chill of autumn in my heart. The light is different this time of year, golden and burnt orange, as if the color of the landscape is reflected in the sky, casting its magical glow. I only wish it would keep me warm. I think the chill in my heart is the sad realization that I will not marry Brom. I have railed against this marriage for so long now I think I forgot why it was I loved him so long ago.

Katrina and Brom sat beneath the Oldest Tree like they did when they were young. Katrina felt a deep sadness in her heart sitting across from him. For the first time in years, she felt at ease and connected to him. As he shared his encounter with the Headless Horseman in vivid detail, she could see the events playing out in her mind, and she could sense he was still filled with a sense of dread and terror. Brom's hands were shaking as he described the Spectral Rider's demon horse nearly crushing his skull. She had never seen him so frightened, or so vulnerable.

"Katrina, *please* don't tell a soul about this, especially not your father. And for goodness' sake, don't tell Ichabod."

Katrina wanted to mention the irony, him being attacked by the Headless Horseman after how mercilessly he teased Ichabod, but she couldn't bring herself to do anything but listen and reassure him. "I won't say a word, Brom, I promise." She wanted to take his hand in hers if only to calm his nerves, and to stop his hand from trembling. She felt her heart softening to him seeing him so vulnerable and wondered if this shift in him would last. "I'm just happy you're all right," she said, feeling sad about the state of things between them. She had loved him so much, and though she felt her heart reaching out to him that afternoon, she couldn't help but remember how awful he had been treating her lately.

"I know you've not been happy with me, Katrina. But I honestly don't understand what I did wrong," he said with the saddest look on his face.

"I'm sorry, Brom. I love you, but I don't want to marry you. I haven't for a long time now. We don't want the same things."

"You mean you want Ichabod!" he said, and as if he had conjured him by speaking his name, Brom turned around to see his nemesis standing on the road. "Speak of the scarecrow." He rolled his eyes, and there he was again, the Brom she couldn't love with her entire heart.

"I'm sorry things turned out this way for us, Brom. Truly I am. I hope one day you find someone who loves you unreservedly," she said as Crane's jaunty voice called out from the road.

"Katrina, my dear!" He was holding a stack of books in one hand and tipping his hat with the other in his usual dandy flourish, bowing at the waist. Brom shook his head and smirked.

"How can you stand him, Katrina?" he said, getting up and dusting off the dry leaves that stuck to his trousers. Katrina could tell that Brom felt uncomfortable and didn't want Ichabod to see him in such a state. He was still wearing the same clothes he wore the night before, which were covered in dirt, and he looked as if he hadn't slept at all.

"You all right there, good man?" said Crane as he headed over.

"I'm fine, Crow. Just leaving."

"I'm sure you'll be happy to know I had no deadly encounters with the Headless Horseman last night, though I suppose my head still being attached to my neck is testament to that account," Crane said, laughing. "Though by the looks of you, I wonder how *you* fared on Sleepy Hollow Road." He looked Brom up and down.

"Good-bye, Katrina. I hope you're happy with your choice," Brom said, turning on his heel and leaving quickly without a word for Crane.

"Good-bye, Brom." Katrina knew she had broken his heart, and she felt as if he had taken a tiny piece of her own heart with him. She kept her eyes on him as he walked slowly down Sleepy Hollow Road, wondering what would become of his life now that they were no longer together. So much of his future was tied up with Katrina and her family. She felt she had not only broken his heart but destroyed his future as well.

"He looks like he's in a sorry state," said Crane with an unusually wicked grin on his face.

"Be sweet, Ichabod, he's going through a hard time right now," replied Katrina, watching Brom and that tiny piece of her heart disappear on the path.

"I should say he is, realizing what he's lost." He kissed her hand. "Your beauty is so bewitching I almost forgot my purpose in venturing here, my dear Katrina. Here, I brought this for you." He handed her a book, but she didn't look at it; her eyes were still on the path even though Brom was no longer in her sight. "Katrina?"

She blinked a few times and refocused on Crane. "I'm so sorry, thank you, Ichabod." She couldn't help but feel worried for Brom.

"Please don't tell me you still have feelings for that imbecile, Katrina. He's a dolt and a bully and doesn't deserve you," said Crane, looking a little peevish.

"Of course I still have feelings for him, Ichabod. We've been close since childhood; feelings like that don't disappear overnight," she said, surprising herself.

"Then you're still in love with him?" he asked, backing away from her, almost recoiling, his goofily charming features now looking gawky and hardened.

"I love him, but not quite as well as I once did. My heart no longer belongs to him." She felt sad to admit it, but it seemed to put Ichabod at ease.

"Then it will be my mission to win your heart, dear Katrina," he said, putting out his arm. "It would be my great pleasure if you would allow me to escort you home."

⌣

After that day, the Oldest Tree became their special meeting place. The two of them would sit under the protection of its branches for hours, talking of their dreams and plans for the future. It's where Katrina shared all the things with Ichabod that she never could with Brom—how she desperately wanted to leave Sleepy Hollow, how she wanted to travel the world, and her most secret desire she hadn't shared with anyone.

"Do you know what I would love most, Ichabod?" she asked one lazy autumn afternoon.

"To spend your life with me," he said, gingerly taking a tiny deep red leaf out of her golden hair. "Because that is what I desire most." And she was suddenly very happy to have a man who encouraged her and respected her for who she was, and most importantly, never tried to force her into a life she didn't want.

"You're so sweet, Ichabod," she said, looking down at the little leaf he placed in her hand. It was so small and delicate, a perfectly shaped leaf in miniature. She opened the book of poems by Byron they had been reading earlier and placed it within its pages. "I was going to say what I would love most is to become an author." As she said it, she hoped he didn't think she sounded foolish.

"I think that's a capital idea, Katrina. I think you would be a captivating author. Do you have a story in mind?" he said, though she couldn't help noticing he did look slightly hurt that her greatest desire wasn't to marry him.

"I think I want to chronicle Sleepy Hollow's ghost stories and legends, especially the Headless Horseman." She felt nervous and thrilled to be sharing this with someone at last.

"And I suppose you'll call it *The Adventures of Ichabod Crane*," he said, laughing. Katrina blinked and shook her head.

"No. What do you mean? Why would I call it that?"

He gave her the queerest look, as if she should know exactly what he was talking about.

"Katrina, my featherheaded darling, you must have forgotten, I told you I was planning to write about my experiences here in Sleepy Hollow. A young school-master making his way in a new town, discovering the secrets of the Headless Horseman."

She searched her mind, trying to recall that conversation. She didn't recall him ever saying such a thing.

"I don't think you told me about this, Ichabod. And for the record, while I admit I do tend to forget things, I don't particularly like being called a featherhead."

Crane frowned. "Oh, my daring, I didn't mean offense. You know I think you are the brightest woman in Sleepy Hollow. But you must remember our conversation, it was the very evening your mama made pecan pie, chocolate bread pudding, and pumpkin tarts for dessert. You remember, we sat on the back porch looking at the stars after dinner."

Katrina sighed. "I remember that night, but I don't recall you mentioning you wanted to write that story."

"Well, that hurts my feelings, Katrina. Everything we talk about burns brightly in my mind like a spark of light that never fades," he said, making her feel bad. "I wonder how many things you've forgotten, my dearest, when I have carefully curated every conversation we've had, like the most dutiful of caretakers. Why, I even remember your favorite fairy tale, the one about the witch who eats the bones of children and flies around in her mortar and pestle. That's what gave me the idea to tell the Headless Horseman's tale, you remember. I said I was surprised you loved such a morbid story, and you said you grew up with such tales like those of the Headless Horseman, and I said I would love to commit his history to paper with my trusted quill."

"I'm sorry, Ichabod," she said, feeling very confused.

"Not to worry, my sweet. I'm sure you will think of a story of your own." He patted her on the head. "Come along, my sweet featherhead. Twilight is upon us, and your family will be cross with us if we are late for dinner."

FOURTEEN

THE GHOST IN THE TREE

The sky was starting to turn golden, with streaks of red clouds, casting an autumnal glow on the Oldest Tree. The leaves danced as if agitated as Kat snapped Katrina's diary closed and threw it, startling Isadora.

"What's wrong, Kat?"

"It was so obvious Crane was lying," Kat said, standing up and pacing back and forth. "I mean, come on! All that stuff about him saying he was going to write about the Headless Horseman. Katrina didn't forget, and I think she knew it; she just didn't want to admit he was being a jerk. And calling her a featherhead? What the hell was that?"

Isadora narrowed her eyes. "I'm sorry, it must be hard reading that after everything Blake has done to you," she said, taking Kat's hand.

"You mean all the stuff I *let* Blake do to me?" said Kat, still angry.

"That's not what I mean at all, Kat."

"All of this is just too weird, right? I mean don't you think? It's like I'm living Katrina's life."

Isadora shook her head. "I'm not sure it's that simple."

"I wonder, though," Kat said, feeling lost in her emotions. She was feeling too many things at once to be able to concentrate clearly. So much had happened in just a couple of days. She was seeing her life clearly for the first time in a while, but she was afraid she hadn't yet gotten control over it, like she was living Katrina's life, and it frightened her. Was she just jumping into another relationship because that was what she was used to? The only thing she knew for certain was that she was happy this was happening with Isadora. She usually felt very alone when she was overwhelmed, but for some reason, she felt she was safe with Isadora. "Let's go, we're going to be late for dinner." She took Isadora by the hand. "Wait, we forgot Katrina's diary." She leaned down to pick up the diary at the base of the tree, and as she stood up, she thought she heard something.

"Do you hear that?" Kat stood stock-still, trying to be as quiet as possible so she could hear. "Shhh, don't move." She put her ear closer to the tree, but the moment she did she scrambled away in terror. "Oh my God! Is that a heartbeat?" Instinctively, she pulled Isadora away from the tree.

"That's the same thing Brom heard the night he saw the Headless Horseman," said Isadora, her voice rising. "We have to go, *now*!" Isadora looked like she might faint. Kat took her by the hand to steady her.

"Shhh, wait!" said Kat. "I think I hear a voice inside." She leaned in closer, trying to bring Isadora with her, but she wouldn't budge, she was too afraid. "Come here, listen, I don't think he's going to hurt us."

"What do you mean *he*? Who isn't going to hurt us?" But before Kat could answer, the tree started to ooze a thick, deep red viscous fluid; it was seeping out of the hollow and pooling at the base. None of this felt real. Kat thought she might faint as well. They both recoiled in horror. Kat felt like they had somehow stepped into the pages of Katrina's diary. The blood flooded the forest floor, covering the leaves and pooling at their feet.

"Wait, look, there is something there," Kat said, pointing out the shining object in the pool of blood a few inches from her foot. She reached down and pulled it out, wiping it off on her long skirt.

"Don't touch it, Kat. *Please* come on!"

"Look, it's a locket." Kat's hand started to tremble as she turned over the hinged golden oval. There, engraved on the other side, were Katrina's initials—*her* initials. "I think it belonged to Katrina." She just stood, sickened by the blood that still clung to it and covered her hands.

"Be calm. I won't hurt you." The voice came from within the tree. It was deep, sonorous, and somehow comforting.

"What the actual what?" she said, dropping the locket. She watched it as it sank out of sight beneath the pool of blood.

"You are entirely safe with me. Years ago, I promised Katrina, the first of her name, that I would always protect those who share her name, and so I shall. Go home and keep reading. I know Katrina wants you to know the truth."

"Where is Katrina? Why doesn't she tell me this herself?"

"Because he won't let her, but you need to know the truth, and she doesn't want you to be afraid."

"Who won't let her? What truth? Who are you?" she asked, feeling like the world was shifting beneath her feet. She felt dizzy and nauseated, and couldn't focus properly. Her vision was becoming narrower, and she was seized by a pain behind her eyes. She was afraid she was going to pass out.

"You must leave, Kat, before he arrives."

"Before who arrives? The Headless Horseman?" she asked, reaching for Isadora to steady herself. She saw flashing, jagged colorful lights in her peripheral vision. She was so disoriented she slumped down on the ground, not caring that she was sitting near the encroaching pool of blood.

"Kat, are you okay?" Isadora sat down next to her, looking into her eyes. "Kat? What's the matter?"

"Neither of you should fear the Horseman. Now please go from here and finish Katrina's story—she wants you both to know how it ends," said the hollow voice in the tree. The heartbeat grew louder, and the blood began to gush around them, soaking through their clothes. Kat felt as if she were drowning in fear, immobilized, her head splitting with pain.

"Kat! Are you okay?" Kat could hear Isadora desperately calling to her, but she was transfixed by the Oldest Tree. She didn't understand why she was so terrified; she felt there was something trapped inside, or someone, and it made her heart pound like thunder, her heartbeat matching the one coming from inside the tree.

"How do we know you're telling the truth?" Kat asked.

"Open the locket."

A clawlike hand reached out from within the hollow, dripping with blood, the locket dangling from a chain around one of its fingers.

"Take it. It was Katrina's. She gave it to me many years ago, but I think now it should belong to you."

Kat reached out and took the locket, but her head was pounding as fast and as hard as her heartbeat.

She put her hands to her head to try to stop the blinding pain as Isadora hugged her tightly, trying to comfort her. "But who *are* you?" she asked, pulling one hand down to open the locket and see Katrina's portrait within.

"I am no one. Now go and read our story. You have awoken me and have set things into motion we may not be able to control. Leave now, before he hurts you. I think he is already upon us."

Then they knew who the voice was talking about. Blake was standing on the road, motionless with shock as he stared at Kat and Isadora standing beneath the Oldest Tree, both of them covered in blood.

FIFTEEN

THE SECRET OF
ISADORA CROW

Isadora and Blake were ordered to sit at the kitchen table to be kept under the watchful eye of Maddie while Trina tended to Kat upstairs in her bedroom.

"What in Sleepy Hollow's Ghost happened out there?" Kat's mother was in a state.

"Mom, I can't think properly right now. Please calm down." Kat's headache was starting to subside, but she was still feeling dizzy and nauseated.

"Calm down? You're telling me to calm down when you show up covered in blood?"

Kat put her hand over her eyes to shield them from the light in the room. "Mom, can we talk about this later? I promise I will tell you everything."

"Of course. You rest. I'm sorry, I'll be back to check

on you," said Trina, turning off the light and leaving the room.

Kat knew Blake and Isadora were downstairs in the kitchen talking to Maddie. She hated the idea of her mom meeting Isadora like this for the first time, and didn't like that she was down there alone with her mom, Maddie, and Blake. Kat got up and opened her bedroom door slightly so she could hear them talking.

"Is Kat okay, Mrs. Van Tassel? Can I go see her?" Kat could hear the fear in Isadora's voice.

"No, you may not, Isadora *Crow,* she is resting. And yes, she will be fine. She's having a migraine that was likely triggered by whatever happened in the Hollow. What she needs now is quiet." Trina poured herself a cup of tea. She sat at the table next to Blake, across from Isadora. "Now tell me what happened." Kat could just picture her mother narrowing her eyes at Isadora over her teacup as she took a sip.

"Yeah, Crow, what happened? Why are you covered in blood?" Blake sounded angry, and Kat was worried about Isadora being down there alone under their interrogation, but she could barely stand and had to use her door frame to steady herself.

"We were reading Katrina's diary when all of a sudden the Oldest Tree started gushing blood and talking to us."

"What did the voice sound like? Was it a woman?" asked Maddie.

"No, it was a man's voice. He kept saying 'He is coming.' I think he was trying to warn us Blake was coming, and the voice in the tree was afraid he was going to hurt us."

"You don't believe this, do you? Why would I ever do anything to hurt Kat?"

"Really, Blake? So, what was the other night about, then? Showing off to your friends, pressuring Kat at the cemetery to summon Katrina and then running off when that horse showed up?"

"What horse? Is this true, Blake?" asked Kat's mother.

Someone had dropped a teacup. Kat heard it shatter on the floor.

"Sleepy Hollow's Ghost! You didn't? What could that girl be thinking, to dishonor her namesake by trying to invoke Katrina's spirit on her night of rest?" said Maddie.

"She didn't want to do it! Blake bullied her into going to the cemetery and tricked her into doing the ceremony even though she didn't want to. It's not her fault."

"And what part did you have in all of this, Isadora *Crow*?" asked Maddie.

"I tried to talk her out of it. I was afraid of what might happen."

"I should think you would be, young lady!" said Maddie so sharply it made Kat flinch. She had never heard Maddie sound so angry before. She wished with all her heart she was down there with Isadora, but she sounded like she was holding her own.

"Yes, Miss *Crow*, we see you clearly. We know who you are. Did you and your family think changing your name to Crow would work? We all knew who you were the moment your family moved to town."

There was a long silence, during which Kat pictured them all looking at Isadora.

"I'm not like him, you know," she said, looking at the bloody diary before her on the table.

"Then why hide who you are from Kat?"

"What's going on? Who is she?" asked Blake, but none of the women answered.

"I was afraid." Isadora kept her eyes trained on the diary, while Trina, Maddie, and Blake all stared at her. "And here you are just like your distant many-times-great uncle, trying to ruin the life of another Katrina," Trina said, slamming her fist on the table. "Well, I won't have it, do you understand me? I won't have you waltzing into Sleepy Hollow and wreaking havoc on our lives! Katrina has a responsibility and a destiny here in Sleepy Hollow, and I won't have you standing in her way."

Isadora looked up and met Trina's eyes. "I'm sorry to say this, but if anyone is standing in her way, it's you. Do you realize how much she wants to go to college? She wants to be a writer, Mrs. Van Tassel, but she doesn't want to disappoint you, even though she is terrified of being stuck in this town forever. Do you understand how deep her fear of being trapped here runs? She has disavowed the existence of the supernatural because she is terrorized by the idea of dying here and becoming one of Sleepy Hollow's ghosts!"

"You're talking nonsense; Kat never mentioned wanting to become a writer, and she doesn't believe in our history because she is being contrary. She's a teenager; that's what you all do!" said Trina, but Maddie took over the conversation.

"I think Miss Crane is right, Trina. Katrina has said as much to me during our talks under the Oldest Tree."

Blake finally spoke up after sitting there looking as if he was trying to work out the greatest of mysteries. "So, Isadora is a Crane?" he blurted out, startling all the ladies at the table.

"Yes, dear, keep up," said Maddie, shaking her head and rolling her eyes.

"*You're a Crane!* Oh, Kat is going to *love* that!" he said sarcastically, leaning back in his chair and laughing. "I told her you were a freak. You realize she won't ever forgive you for lying. Not ever," he said, with a sinister smile on his face.

"I'm sure you're right. I have a feeling Kat has had enough lying for a lifetime after being in a relationship with you. I honestly wouldn't blame her if she didn't speak to either of us ever again," Isadora said, tears now trickling down her face.

"You're right, Isadora Crane."

It was Kat, standing in the kitchen doorway. "I don't want to speak to either of you again." She turned around to leave but decided she had more to say.

"And, both of you, *beware of the Headless Horseman.*"

SIXTEEN

ICHABOD CRANE HIGH

Tensions at school were high on Wednesday, and Kat was thankful they were about to take their autumn break. Crane High was different from other schools. Their seasonal breaks coincided with the various harvests, the most important of which in Sleepy Hollow was the Autumn Harvest, which the town celebrated with the festival and the ball on All Hallows' Eve. This was Kat's favorite time of year, because the extended fall break meant they weren't at school long before the winter harvest break. This meant they didn't have a long summer vacation like traditional schools to accommodate their light schedule during fall and winter, but summer wasn't Kat's favorite season anyway.

She had completely forgotten she had final exams this week. She'd likely have to make some of them up since her mom and dad insisted she stay home Monday and Tuesday to recover from the events over the weekend. She was glad, because she wasn't ready to face everyone at school, especially Blake and Isadora. As she sat at the end of her bed, she couldn't help but feel like she was living Katrina's life. Was there some sort of Van Tassel curse? Or did reading the diary set these events in motion? And who was this woman who was haunting her? She had so many questions, none of which she had time to think about. She had to get ready for school.

She opened her phone to look at her schedule on the school app. While her school schedule loaded, an animation played of the Headless Horseman slinging his flaming jack-o'-lantern head at a gangly depiction of Ichabod Crane.

"This is all a joke to them," she muttered, shaking her head. "My life is a joke. I got taken in by a Crane just like Katrina did."

It felt like a lifetime since she had been to school last. So much had happened in the span of a weekend, it was hard for Kat to wrap her head around the idea that her life had completely turned upside down in the space of a handful of days. In the two days she had stayed home, everyone at school had time to talk about what had happened at the cemetery, and her breakup with Blake.

"Are you sure you're up to going to school?" Kat's dad had asked earlier that morning. He had stayed home from work both days that week, worried sick over Kat. He had been working long hours during the fall harvest, and when he got home Sunday night and heard what had happened, he was beside himself with anger and worry. "I hate seeing you like this, Kat. I don't understand why you didn't tell us sooner what was going on with Blake. I want to smash that boy's head in like a pumpkin. I told him he isn't allowed in this house ever again." Kat grabbed her father's hand; she felt loved unconditionally, and supported, and it was a magical feeling.

"I guess I didn't tell you because I didn't fully see what he was doing, not at first anyway," she said, realizing it was much more complicated than that.

"It feels like you've been trying to tell us this for a long time, Kat, and I feel awful I wasn't listening." Kat wanted to cry seeing her dad look so vulnerable and so sorry.

"Oh, Dad, I love you so much, but it's not your fault."

Kat's dad hugged her tightly in his arms. "Blake had us all fooled; I feel like an idiot not seeing who he really was."

Kat smirked. She felt the same way.

"He was good at that, though, putting on a good show for you and Mom," she said, remembering how attentive and sweet he'd be in their company.

"So, it's ended between you, then, you're not going to let him talk you into staying together?"

Kat understood why he asked that. She had told her parents everything. It was like a great gush of words, and emotion poured out of her when she finally started talking; it was like she couldn't stop once she had started. She saw that they were overwhelmed and confused, but most importantly, she felt they believed her, and that's what mattered most.

"No, Dad. I won't let him talk me into anything ever again," she said, tears falling down her cheeks.

"And what about Isadora? How do you feel about her now? Do you think you'll give her another chance?" She was surprised he asked this.

"She lied to me, Dad. How can I ever trust her again?"

Kat's dad clasped his hands together and rested them on his chin like he often did when he was trying to find the right words.

"She was afraid, Kat. Look how your mom and Maddie reacted when they found out you two became friends. Of course she lied about who she really was, this is Sleepy Hollow, for goodness' sake; everyone hates the Cranes. But it seems to me she's been a really good friend, maybe even more than a friend?" he asked with a wide grin that made her heart happy and skip a beat.

"How did you know I have feelings for her?"

"Kat, I know you. I've seen how you look when you talk about her, and so did your mom and Maddie; that's why they were so concerned. But, Kat, I'd hate for you to turn your back on someone who seems to really care about you, just because you're afraid." Her dad was right; she was afraid.

"Then you think I can trust her?"

Her dad smiled. "There's only one way to find out, my sweet girl."

Kat cried all the tears she was crying for so many reasons, but most of all because her dad was being so amazing.

"I love you, Dad," she said, looking at the clock and realizing she was going to be late. "I better get ready for school."

Her dad gave her another hug. "I love you, too, my girl. Text me or your mom if you want to come home early." He flashed her his brilliant smile and gave her one of his bear hugs before leaving her room. She couldn't believe she just had that conversation with her dad; it took her completely by surprise. Life had felt so surreal over the past several days, and she was still trying to grasp her new reality.

When she had opened her closet that morning to take out her school uniform, a sense of dread washed over her. After everything that happened, going back to school felt daunting, and her school felt even more ludicrous than ever. Even the uniforms were laughable, all black with orange ties and flaming jack-o'-lantern patches on their cardigans.

It had never made sense to Kat that their school was named after the most ridiculed and reviled man in the history of Sleepy Hollow, but since Ichabod Crane had founded the school and Sleepy Hollow cherished its history so well, they named the school after him, a cautionary tale for those who didn't take the Legend of

Sleepy Hollow seriously. It had all been sort of a joke to Kat, considering the kids in school didn't seem to take the story very seriously, and she didn't feel the education she was receiving in Sleepy Hollow was adequately preparing her for college.

Kat hated her high school more than ever now and dreaded the thought of running into Isadora or Blake, or anyone really. She didn't particularly care for most of the people she went to school with, especially Blake's friends. They had never really been *her* friends, and she had always felt the only reason they hung out with her was because she was Blake's girlfriend. Now that this was no longer true, they didn't have a reason to talk to her at all, which was fine with her. It was strange, but she felt less alone now than she did when she was with Blake. Though she wished things had turned out differently with Isadora. She hadn't realized how much she wanted someone in her life that loved the same things she did until she met Isadora that night at the cemetery gates. She replayed all their conversations over and over in her mind, and she knew the exact moments Isadora wanted to tell her the truth, and how she agonized over it, but Kat couldn't bring herself to trust her. She was afraid she was going from one gaslighter to another.

And there was a part of her that had felt all along it was too soon to get involved with someone else. She wanted time to get to know herself again, to become a person she liked and respected. She wanted to be her own person, and not just someone's girlfriend. She didn't want to jump into another relationship because she was afraid to be alone.

Kat finally got her schedule to load on the app, and she saw there were no finals that day, but she had missed her Historical Events exam, and Headmaster Toad had emailed requesting she come to his office the day she returned to school.

Once she got to school, she headed to the headmaster's office and saw a group of students clustered around a locker, all of them with their cell phones out, presumably taking photos of whatever was happening at the locker. She sighed as she walked past them, through the gardens, and up the wide marble steps that led to the massive Greek Revival building with fluted columns. The entryway was flanked by two life-size black iron statues: To the left was the Headless Horseman, and to the right was Ichabod Crane, hat in hand as he fled the dark rider and his demon horse.

As she entered the building, she was struck by the

enormous fountain in the center of the room, a statue of the first Katrina under the Oldest Tree. The light coming in from the massive paned-glass dome overhead sparkled on the rippling water, making the statue seem alive. She had walked past this fountain daily for the past three years and never once had she appreciated its significance. Kat stood there looking at the statue of Katrina, and for the first time, she felt like she truly knew her, and had in fact carried something of her within herself. All she thought about while she was recovering was how uncanny it was that she seemed to be living a life parallel to her ancestor's.

She shook off her musings finally and made her way to the headmaster's office. His assistant always reminded Kat of a badger, with his long, pointed nose and small square spectacles. He wore the same green tweed suit every day, with a red-and-gold scarf to ward off the chill in the large drafty building.

"Good morning, Mr. Angus. Headmaster Toad wants to see me?" she said, making the twitchy man jump with fright.

"Yes, yes, of course, Miss Van Tassel, the headmaster is expecting you. Go right in," he said in his usual nervous manner. Kat always found the headmaster to be rather jovial, so she wondered why his assistant was always so jumpy and nervous. She couldn't imagine Headmaster Toad was an overly demanding boss, or hard on the poor fellow—in fact he was often away on various road trips. Nevertheless, Mr. Angus was always in a state of agitation.

"Thank you, Mr. Angus," she said as she opened the large wooden door.

"Well, hello, Katrina," said the headmaster as she entered his office. He always used her given name, which usually annoyed her, but not on this day. Today she felt like a Katrina. "I was sorry to hear you've been unwell, but I do hope you find yourself revived and feeling fit to take your autumn finals." He pushed a large glass jar in her direction, filled with hard candies in crinkly plastic wrappers. "Take one, take one! You're in for a wild ride this afternoon with two exams to make up!" he said.

"I only saw one on the schedule, Headmaster Toad," she said, eyeing the bronze statue of a frog on his desk that looked as if he was eager for a piece of the candy the headmaster had just offered her.

"Perhaps I was mistaken, dear. Let me check," he said, clicking away on his computer. "Oh yes, I see, yes, there we go, you missed your written exam for Historical Events yesterday, so I suggest you take your free periods to make up the written exam and to prepare for the oral exam at the end of the day today." He gave her a wide grin that made his eyes look unusually large and froglike.

"Thank you, Headmaster Toad, though I wonder why I didn't just arrange this with Professor Cyril." She wished she hadn't come back to school. The last thing she wanted to do was stand in front of the class after everything that happened. The thought of it was making her heart race, and she was starting to feel as if she might be getting another migraine and wondered if she shouldn't just text her dad to pick her up.

"Katrina, dear, is that your phone? You know I ask all students to silence their phones before entering my office." Kat hadn't even noticed her alerts were blowing up. She didn't bother to look at the screen before she turned off the ringer.

"I'm so sorry," she said, eyeing the bronze frog, who was eyeing the candy.

"Please take a piece on your way out, dear. I know you have a lot to do today," he said, standing up to dismiss her. "Good luck on your exams, Katrina. I know how much you would like to make the first Katrina proud," he added as she made her way out the door.

She felt exhausted, heartbroken, and weary. The last thing she wanted to do was take her exams, but she made her way to the library, where she usually spent her free periods.

The library was her favorite spot at school. It was quiet and filled with the scent of old books. She took a few off the shelf and found herself a cozy chair in a nook near a window with sunlight to keep her warm. She had forgotten how cold it was in the main building, or else she wouldn't have left her school cloak at home, which she often did because she thought they were ridiculous and old-fashioned. But that was Sleepy Hollow—ridiculous and old-fashioned.

She went over her notes from previous Historical Events classes and found some ideas she'd jotted down of what she wanted to write about for the exam. None of them seemed interesting to her any longer. Professor Cyril suggested they pick their own topic, only specifying that it must be about Sleepy Hollow. Then it hit her: She would write about the night Ichabod Crane was run

out of town after the Harvest Ball, but she would tell
the story from Katrina's point of view. So, she took out
Katrina's diary, which she had tucked away in her book
bag, excited to read the rest of the story. And then she
felt a pang that Isadora wasn't there to read it with her.

"What did you say about me to all of your stupid
friends?" Kat looked up from the diary to see Isadora
standing next to her. Isadora's eyes were swollen and red,
and her eyeliner was smudged.

"I don't know what you're talking about. I don't have
any friends," she said.

"Well, you told someone." Isadora could hardly
speak she was crying so hard.

"Told someone *what?*" Kat asked. Isadora just stared
as she handed Kat her phone, open to a photo of her
locker.

"I'm so sorry, I didn't know. I've been in the
headmaster's office. I promise I didn't say anything to
anyone," said Kat as Isadora wiped her tears on the
sleeve of her sweater, smearing her eyeliner more.

"Then you said something to Blake. I mean, why
would they write that on my locker? Is that how people
feel here?" She pulled at the sleeves of her cardigan,

trying to make them longer so they covered her hands. It looked like she was trying to make herself as small as possible so she could disappear.

"I swear I didn't say anything to Blake. He's the last person I would talk to about my feelings for you."

"You still have feelings for me?"

"I do, but you lied to me. I've never felt this way about anyone, but before I could even figure out what this is, I find out you've been lying about who you are. You just sat there not saying a word when I told you about all the horrible things Blake did to me, how he lied and manipulated me. For the first time, I felt safe sharing my feelings with someone, and then I find out they're not even who I thought they were."

Isadora crossed her arms across her chest, looking as if she needed protection from Kat's words.

"I'm sorry I lied. I'm so sorry. I wanted to tell you, I really did, especially that day at the tree. I like you so much, Kat, I didn't want anything to ruin it, but I guess I screwed things up anyway." She walked away before Kat could say anything more.

Kat wanted to go after her, and almost did. She wanted to more than anything. She wanted to say she was sorry someone wrote those horrible things on her locker, she wanted to say she understood why she was afraid, she wanted to say all the things, but that's what she always did. She took care of people who hurt her feelings. She did it for years with Blake and she wasn't going to do it again. She thought about when Isadora broke down at the Oldest Tree, and she was sure Isadora was going to tell her the truth that day before they heard that noise in the hollow. She saw every other time Isadora tried to tell her the truth sparking vividly in her memory. And in that moment, she wondered if she could find a way to truly trust her. And then she remembered what her father said: *I'd hate for you to turn your back on someone who seems to really care about you, just because you're afraid.*

But she was afraid. So instead of going after Isadora she opened Katrina's diary.

SEVENTEEN

THE DIARY OF KATRINA VAN TASSEL

MR. CROW'S
MISCALCULATION

To hear my mother tell it, my father, Baltus, lived in fear of spending time alone with Ichabod Crane, especially since he and I have become so inseparable. Ichabod had been joining us for dinner most every evening, and he had been spending his free days with me, doting upon my every wish, until finally, to my father's horror, he worked up his courage to ask for my hand in marriage. And long after that fateful night, when my papa and I were alone together talking, he told me how he felt, and exactly how it all happened.

⁀

Though the gangly Mr. Crane wasn't Baltus's first choice in a husband for his daughter, he could tell Katrina was happier than he'd ever seen her. So he couldn't help but feel nervous when he found himself in the dining room after dinner alone with the dreaded Mr. Crane while Katrina and Regina were preparing dessert in the kitchen.

"May I offer you a glass of port, Crow?" Baltus asked, taking the stopper out of the decanter and then pouring himself a glass.

"I would be delighted to partake in a libation with you, good sir," he said, making Baltus roll his eyes. This was just the sort of thing he hated about Ichabod; he wasn't capable of a simple answer.

Though Baltus was a simple man, that shouldn't be mistaken for unintelligent, and he was almost sure Crane had made that mistake. It was really no matter to Baltus. He didn't care what a pretentious schoolteacher thought of him, but he did care what Crane thought of his daughter, and by all accounts, he seemed to respect and value Katrina's mind as well as her beauty. Just that night, he had been boasting about what a compelling author she could be. And though Baltus was pleased his daughter was so happy, he did long for the days when he and Regina thought Katrina would marry Brom, another person he was sure Crane underestimated.

Baltus hated seeing Brom in such a sorry way. He hadn't been his usual jovial self since the night he and Baltus gave Ichabod such a hard time about the Headless Horseman. Something in Brom changed after that night, and no matter how Baltus pressed, Brom wouldn't say a word. When he asked Katrina, all she would say was that it was over between them, and he had to assume the young man was just smarting, even though Baltus's instincts said there was more to the story.

He wished things hadn't progressed so quickly with Crane and Katrina, else Baltus could have helped his daughter and Brom to find their way back to each other. If only Katrina could see how much he had changed, for he was sure Katrina still cared for Brom deeply, and there might have been a chance for them if Crane hadn't pranced onto the scene like a scarecrow on stilts.

Baltus missed having Brom to dinner; he missed their conversations, discussing their plans for the future, and most especially his company. He found himself grieving for the life he had planned for them as a family, and he knew in his heart Brom was feeling the same way.

"You look as if something is bothering you, Mr. Van Tassel," said Crane, trying to break the tension in the room.

"Indeed, there is, Mr. Crow," he said, knowing full well he was calling him by the wrong name. It was one of his rare pleasures while having to suffer so many evenings with a man he disliked when he'd rather be at the pub with Brom laughing and joking.

"Perhaps then my query will bring you out of your dark and brooding mood," said Crane, taking the decanter and pouring himself a glass of port. "Though I think I need a bit of courage before I jump off the metaphoric cliff, you might say." Crane gulped down the entire glass of port and poured himself another.

"I doubt that is something I would say," scoffed Baltus, and Crane laughed.

"I dare say you are right, good man," said Crane, not realizing Baltus understood his comment to its full extent. "Mr. Van Tassel, might I be so brave as to ask for your enchanting daughter's hand in marriage?" he inquired, clutching his hand to his chest like a dramatic stage actor, and it was all Baltus could do not to burst out laughing at this ridiculous man.

"I don't know, Crow; only you can answer that," Baltus said, clearly catching Crane off guard.

"I do believe I am, good sir. I take the highest risk because I know you do not approve of me." He clutched his chest even more dramatically, rumpling the lapels of his jacket.

"You're right, Mr. Crow, I do have my doubts about you. I wonder what will become of Katrina's legacy, and I fear for the future of Sleepy Hollow should you be unable to run the farm and estate. Most people in this county are in my employ or count upon our crops for their income. I know Katrina wants to travel the world, and while I am happy she is in love with someone who encourages her dreams, I had hoped she would marry someone who could make a happy life for her here, where she is needed most." Baltus was surprised he was sharing so much with this man, but it seemed Crane would soon be his son-in-law and he needed to know the responsibility that came along with marrying into this family.

"But that is exactly what I intend to do, Mr. Van Tassel. Of course I encourage what will make Katrina happiest, but young women, as you know, are fickle, so I have no doubt she will see the wisdom in staying in Sleepy Hollow, especially after we are married and she has settled into her role as wife and mother."

Baltus narrowed his eyes, wondering what this young man was playing at.

"Do you mean to tell me you have no intention of traveling the world with my Katrina, that this is all lies to win her heart?" he said, starting to get angry.

"No, not at all. I will always encourage what makes her happiest, dear man," Crane said. Baltus had to admit there was a part of him that felt better knowing Crane may end up encouraging her to stay, though something about this still put his mind ill at ease.

"The choice is Katrina's, of course," he said, "and I will support what makes her happiest, but, *Crane*, make sure your intentions are clear. Do not make promises to my daughter you don't intend to keep. Do not be false with her in any way." He heard Regina and Katrina coming down the hall.

"Thank you, Mr. Van Tassel. I assure you, I have the best of intentions for your daughter," Crane said, then added with a bit more of his usual dramatic flair, "Now prepare yourself, good sir, for an additional celebration on the eve of the Harvest Ball, because that is when I plan to make my intentions known to our dear Katrina."

Baltus frowned but tried to right his expression when Katrina and her mother came into the room with trays of dessert and coffee. He took a deep breath as he looked at his daughter, realizing she would soon become a married woman, and he knew things would never be the same again.

EIGHTEEN

THE GHOST OF
SLEEPY HOLLOW

Kat stopped reading the diary. Her own father and Katrina's were so much alike. She kept hearing her father's words again and again, tugging on her heart. She wished more than ever she had gone after Isadora, and felt terrible she didn't comfort her. She was so afraid of going from one bad relationship to the next, from one person who had lied to her to another. Then she felt a hand on her shoulder. She thought it was Isadora, and it made her smile, but when she looked up, no one was there.

"You can trust her, Kat, and trust the voice in the tree. My story concerns you both."

Kat stood up, knocking over her chair, making a loud clatter. "Katrina?" She spun around in circles looking for her but didn't see anyone, even though she had the familiar chill and feeling of being watched again, and it wasn't just the other students in the library giving her strange looks and whispering behind their hands. She scanned the room looking for her; she knew she was there somewhere, and then she saw her standing under the arched doorway of the library, transparent and glowing like an overexposed photograph from the light of the sun coming through the domed skylight above.

"Come with me, Kat. She is at our tree. Go to her before it's too late," said the wraith. Kat couldn't see her clearly but she had a very real sense that it was Katrina. The ghostly woman walked away, leaving Kat to hastily shove her things into her bag. When she got out of the library, she saw the woman a few yards ahead, walking silently toward Sleepy Hollow Grove.

When they got to the Oldest Tree, Kat was reminded how she felt the first time she saw Isadora sitting there beneath its branches, and how she wanted nothing more than to kiss her that day, but she was afraid—she was afraid of losing herself again in another relationship, and she was afraid of being hurt even though there was something that told her she could trust Isadora.

"She lied to me, Katrina. How do you know I can

trust her?" Kat wished she could see Katrina clearly; she was an indistinguishable fuzzy glow, but what *was* clear was her lilting and comforting voice.

"Trust your heart, Kat. Your heart told you what it needed to hear when you were with Blake and you didn't pay attention. Will you not heed its call now when you've found someone who truly cares for you?"

But before she could answer, Katrina's image drifted away as if it were smoke, dancing away on the breeze that swept through the hollow.

Isadora stood up when she saw Kat coming down the road. She looked sad and heartbroken, anguished by her regret. There was so much Kat wanted to say to her, but when she saw Isadora's face, her eyes so swollen from crying, she knew what she needed to do was listen, to Isadora and to her heart.

"I'm sorry I lied to you, Kat. I know I should have told you the moment we met, but I was afraid you wouldn't want to be my friend because I'm a Crane. I wanted so much to tell you, especially after we started reading Katrina's diary, and we became . . . closer. I didn't want to lose . . . whatever this is. I tried to tell you so many times, I just couldn't." Isadora buried her face in her hands, sobbing.

"I know, I know, you tried to tell me, I believe you," said Kat, wrapping her arms around Isadora while she cried into her chest.

"I'm so sorry I hurt you. Will you ever find a way to trust me again?" Isadora's face was covered in tears and her heart was aching with regret.

"I think I can trust you," said Kat, wiping Isadora's tears with the cuff of her sweater.

"Do you think you can ever forgive me?"

"I believe I already have," she said as she tenderly took Isadora's face in her hands and kissed her. The kiss was beautiful, perfect, and magical. Pure bliss.

"So, you like girls now? That's disgusting." They hadn't noticed Blake, who had walked up and stood right behind them. Both girls just stood there unable to reply. "Did you see what they wrote on your lockers? Your nasty little secret is out now," he said, showing them a photo on his phone. Kat said nothing even though she wanted to scream at him, tell him every single way he made her feel small, stupid, and insane, but she couldn't. It was like a dangerous storm brewing inside her, and she was afraid to let it out for fear she couldn't control it.

"You have nothing to say for yourself, then? You don't deny it?" He walked toward them. Kat felt trapped, and then she realized she had been trapped with him for as long as she could remember. Trapped in his lies, and trapped in a version of herself she hated. "Clearly you don't care what everyone thinks of you, or how you've made me look." He kept walking closer. "I always knew, you know. It was obvious. I knew you didn't like guys; that's why you treated me like crap. All this time you really wanted to be with a girl. And I knew the moment you met Isadora you liked her. I could see the disgusting way you looked at her."

"Shut the hell up, Blake!" Isadora said, advancing on him, but Kat pulled her back.

"What makes you think I don't like guys?" asked Kat, taking Isadora's hand. "Why can't I like both? This isn't about not liking guys; it's about not liking you!"

"I suppose now you're going to dump me, for *her*, *a Crane*! You realize you're making the same mistake the first Katrina did, and look how that turned out," he said, picking up Katrina's diary, shaking it violently. "I know Katrina has been telling you lies about me since we were young; I know she's behind all of this. She's pushing you toward Isadora. She always hated me. She always warned me not to hurt you."

Kat didn't answer him; she simply snatched the diary back, catching him off guard. She was trying to take this all in. She had felt the inklings of truth coming to her over the past few days, but now it had all come together for her.

"The ghost lady with the blond hair, the one that would follow us around—it was Katrina."

"I thought you didn't believe in ghosts," he said, making his face passive and innocent, pretending he was confused. Kat ignored him. She saw it all now, the reason he'd lied to her all this time.

"You pretended she didn't exist because you didn't want me to believe her. You were afraid she saw you for who you really are."

"Why would I have asked you to you conjure her ghost in the cemetery if I were afraid of her?" he asked, starting to get defensive again.

"Because you knew she would be trapped—you made sure of it by salting the entrance of her crypt. What were you going to do, banish her?" Isadora took Kat by the hand and backed away from him.

"Why would I do that?" he asked.

"Why did you do anything? Maybe you wanted me to feel alone, or make me feel stupid, belittle me, make me doubt myself. Like I was losing my mind, or perhaps you did it just to see if you could manipulate me? Pick one, Blake; any one of them could be true," Kat said, feeling the weight of the truth in her words lifted from her heart, and she felt for the first time she could really breathe.

"That's not true, Kat. I love you! I have been trying to protect you! Don't you see *she's* the one who has been lying to you?" He pointed at Isadora. "Her and Katrina. This is their fault," he said, breaking down and crying. "I love you more than anything in this world; you just make it so hard because no matter what I do you don't believe me. It's like you don't want to be happy."

Both of the girls grimaced.

"Oh, this is just gross," Isadora cut in. "Come on, Kat. Let's go."

"You think Kat will be happy with you, Crow? She can't be happy with anyone!"

Kat had heard this so many times from Blake, and she had actually believed him, but not this time.

"No, Blake, I just can't be happy with you! Goodbye." And for the first time, she didn't have to talk herself into feeling like everything would be okay, because she knew it would be.

She was another step closer to liking herself again.

⌣

Kat and Isadora were sitting on Kat's front porch. There were stacks of pumpkins, large bolts of tulle, black netting, piles of plastic skeletons, and all manner of decorations waiting for someone to bring them to life. With everything going on, she had forgotten Halloween was almost upon them. Maddie, her mother, and the extra staff she hired for the season had been making up for lost time preparing for the Harvest Ball.

"You were pretty incredible just now, everything you said to Blake. You were amazing," Isadora said.

Kat took Isadora's hand and just squeezed it. Isadora didn't know what to say. She was just happy Kat had finally had it out with Blake.

"Should I be here? It looks like things are hectic around here, and I don't think your mom likes me."

"I think she and Maddie are coming around to the idea," Kat said as her mom came out to the porch with cups of hot chocolate.

"Hello, girls. You can drink this out here in the cold,

or come inside," said Trina, smiling at both of them. "I'd love to sit and visit with you ladies, but I have so much to do to prepare for the ball," she said, handing them their cups.

"Let me help you, Mrs. Van Tassel," said Isadora.

"No, dear, you keep Kat here company. You two have been through so much, I want you both to relax," she said, putting her hand on Isadora's shoulder.

"Thank you, Mrs. Van Tassel," Isadora said with a small voice, still feeling a bit sheepish around Kat's mom.

"Please call me Trina. And don't stay out here too long; it's getting cold. Besides, you'll soon be in the way when the staff gets to decorating this porch. Why don't you two visit in the library? You'll be out of the way there, and I'll bring you both something to eat later," she said as she went inside.

"What was that?" Isadora looked surprised Kat's mom was being so nice. She was sure she would never be welcome in the Van Tassel house again.

"We spent a lot of time talking over the past couple of days," Kat said, giving Isadora a quick kiss.

"And they're cool with me? I mean not only being a Crane, but with *us*. I mean, fine with . . . whatever this is." She looked so nervous, Kat kissed her right there on the porch.

"Yeah, they're totally fine with it," she said, laughing. "My parents aren't like Blake and his friends. And for the record, I'm looking forward to finding out what this is," Kat added, giving her another quick kiss.

"Let's go read inside. Your mom was right; it's getting really cold," said Isadora, standing up and then holding out her hand for Kat to take it as she got up.

"That's a good idea. Katrina is eager we finish reading her diary."

"What do you mean?" Isadora dropped Kat's hand, and her eyes grew big.

"I didn't have a chance to tell you because Blake showed up. She came to me in the library and reminded me she wanted us both to read it. She is the one who brought me to you. She said I could trust you," said Kat, taking Isadora's hand back.

"You can trust me, Kat Van Tassel; I promise you." Isadora flashed her magnificent dimples, making Kat want to kiss them. And Kat knew in her heart she could trust her. There was no lingering doubt; she felt at last she was directing her own fate, even if the first Katrina was showing her the way.

NINETEEN

THE DIARY OF KATRINA VAN TASSEL

THE HARVEST BALL

I looked forward to the Harvest Ball with the greatest of expectations, my imagination conjuring a magical and romantic evening. But what happened that night exceeded my wildest daydreams, changing the course of my life in ways I could never have fathomed.

⌇

The Van Tassels' fall Harvest Ball was the most anticipated event in Sleepy Hollow. Everyone in the county would attend, even if it was just to come by for a slice of Regina's famous pumpkin pie, a quick cup of her spiced apple cider, or to stay until the wee hours dancing in the front parlor, and later retiring to the solarium to tell ghost stories. It was a singularly spectacular event, orchestrated by Regina and the staff she hired from the next county over to help with the decorating, food preparation, extra carriages, and various other needs, so no one in Sleepy Hollow would need to work on the night of the ball.

The people of Sleepy Hollow made the majority of their annual income at the fall harvest and the festival that followed, which was held the last two weeks of October. As with most years, the festival had been a tremendous success for everyone in town, and they were looking forward to celebrating another fruitful harvest and festival.

Sleepy Hollow was famed for their pumpkins of different varieties: white fairy-tale pumpkins, so called because they resembled Cinderella's carriage; heirloom pumpkins that looked as if they were grown in a secret magical garden; a sweet sugar-pie variety for baking and cooking; and, of course, orange carving pumpkins of almost every size.

People from all over flocked to Sleepy Hollow to pick out their pumpkins, piling them by the cartful to take home and carve into jack-o'-lanterns. The tourists also enjoyed the various stalls with handmade preserves, pumpkin pies, tarts, caramel apples, popcorn balls, and

Regina's famous cookies. Aside from the delicious home-made goods, the other attractions the visitors seemed to like most were guided tours in horse-drawn buggies, where drivers would regale them with Sleepy Hollow's most famous ghost stories, sending the riders into fits of delight and sometimes terror. The town went all out for the festival, and the Harvest Ball was their way to celebrate and decompress once the festival was over.

Regina had planned the ball down to the last detail and made sure it was executed beautifully and seamlessly. She had arranged for open carriages to bring guests in intervals from the gate at the main road through the oak grove, which was draped with gossamer that danced in the breeze like ghosts and shone in the moonlight, as if they had their own stories to share. Down the center of the oak grove was a dirt path flanked with glowing jack-o'-lanterns portraying all manner of expressions, and Katrina imagined they were listening intently to the ghosts' stories, enraptured by their tales.

As the party guests exited their carriages, they walked down a path lit by lanterns woven into the branches, guiding their way to a mock cemetery featuring tombstones etched with the names of Sleepy Hollow's founders and their most famous residents.

Katrina loved watching everyone step out of their carriages from her balcony, seeing the smiles on their faces
when they saw the decorations, and the children bolt-
ing away with squeals of delight to run and play in the
cemetery.

After traversing the cemetery, the guests were greeted
by a bubbling cauldron over an open fire surrounded by
a group of women dressed as witches singing along with
a small band of musicians dressed as skeletons playing a
mournful dirge. Her mother planned all of this herself,
somehow managing to make each year distinct from the
last and special in its own way, and Katrina wondered
who would continue this tradition if she decided to follow her desire to travel the world. She felt a pang in her
heart at the thought of leaving all of this behind, and
though she had railed against her fate for so long, it was
the future she had envisioned, and she suddenly felt sad
she had to give this up to follow her own dreams.

As she stood on her balcony, she marveled at the
decorations this year. Her mother had adorned the
porch railings with black netting, and on each post
were glowing jack-o'-lanterns with surprising looks on
their faces. The second- and third-floor balconies were
bedecked with fluttering black bats fashioned out of

gauze, featuring gold buttons for eyes that shined in the
dim lamplight that illuminated the balconies.

Inside, the Van Tassel home was also decorated
beautifully with more black and orange netting along
the stair railings and landings, wreaths made of bundles
of autumn flowers and leaves, decorative gourds, and
bundles of colorful corn.

The house was lit entirely by candlelight, both
in the chandeliers and by the jack-o'-lanterns placed
artfully around the home. But the main feature was
the tables laden with heaps of food—a variety rang-
ing from savory to sweet that guests could eat at their
leisure. Regina had a talent of remembering everyone's
favorites and made a point of never letting her guests
go home disappointed or with an empty stomach. She
had prepared her usual array of savory dishes of roast
beef, baked chicken, buttered carrots, meat pies, roasted
pork, and rosemary potatoes, but her favorite and most
artful display was the sweets table, featuring candied
and caramel apples on sticks, colorful popcorn balls,
chocolate-covered-marshmallow ghosts, dark chocolate
cupcakes filled with cherry preserves and topped with
cream cheese frosting, pumpkin tarts, and, of course,
her delicious pies.

Katrina made her way inside and stood on the first-floor landing, which had a view of the vestibule. She was impressed not only by what a remarkable job her mother and the staff had done, but by the magnificent array of costumes worn by their party guests. Most of the women wore voluminous dresses cinched tightly at the waist, and donned whimsical and frightening masks, while others dressed in more elaborate costumes they had clearly been working on all year. Mrs. Irving fashioned herself a pair of bat wings she wore with a black beaded dress, and artfully did her hair in two buns to resemble bat ears, and Mr. Irving had made a very realistic wolf costume, the most impressive feature being its glowing red eyes. She knew immediately he was dressed as a Muckle Black Tyke, a black spectral dog from Scottish fairy tales and myth. She knew this because Mr. Irving spoke of them almost constantly and took every opportunity to share his knowledge of them with anyone who would listen.

Katrina had decided to dress as Mary Read, the lady pirate who donned men's clothing, though she took some liberties with her outfit, asking her mother to make her pirate coat a bit more like a dress, which she wore with men's trousers and black boots that looked fitting for a pirate. Her mother had even managed to find some rather natty-looking gold boot buckles to add some flair to her outfit. She also donned a jaunty pirate hat bursting with red feather plumes and a wide leather belt with a large golden buckle that added volume to her skirted pirate coat. She was happy with her outfit and couldn't wait to see what her guests thought of it.

As Katrina watched the guests pour in, she saw Brom walk into the vestibule with her father. Neither of them was dressed in costume, but they both looked rather smart in their finest Sunday clothes, usually reserved for special occasions. She had forgotten how handsome Brom could be when he wasn't in his work clothes and covered in dirt from being in the fields all day. She suddenly started to feel guilty for how she had gone about things with Brom, turning her affections to Crane so quickly, and not really talking with Brom about how she had been feeling. But she had been dis-enchanted with him for so long, it felt like the next logical step, and she feared it was all a bit of a shock to Brom when she finally ended things.

In the weeks leading up to the ball, she hadn't seen Brom except in passing on Sleepy Hollow Road, or while they were preparing for the festival. It didn't feel quite right not speaking to him, not telling him what was going on in her life, not sharing the new books she had read, or the story ideas she was dreaming up, or even laughing about the stacks of pies tottering on every surface of their kitchen.

"Katrina, dear, you look fantastic!" said a voice from behind her. It was her mother, who stood beside her on the landing.

"Thank you, Mama. You do, too, but do you think anyone will know who you are?" she asked, surprised by her mother's costume. She was dressed as Marie Antoinette, with a giant powdered wig, French court makeup, costume jewelry, and an exquisitely elaborate dress. Her mother had gone all out. Katrina found her mother's costume choice amusing considering her mother was so dearly beloved by everyone in the community. Though they *had* just been reading about what was happening in France and Katrina supposed that's what inspired her costume idea, she knew not everyone in Sleepy Hollow followed the worldly news as closely as she did. Then again, most people probably wouldn't know whom she was dressed as herself, and it would be half the fun of the evening, sharing what she knew about lady pirates to anyone who would listen.

"What are you doing up here, Katrina? Why haven't you gone down and joined the party?" asked her mother.

"Just enjoying watching everyone come in, and I was thinking about Brom. I feel a bit guilty about how I handled things," she said, watching him and her father talk while they drank spiced cider no doubt spiked with whiskey.

"Brom acted like a fool, Katrina. I feel sorry for him, too, honestly, and you know I love him like a son, but you deserve a man who is going to treat you well, someone who appreciates how unique and special you are and encourages you to do the things you love, even if it means leaving Sleepy Hollow to travel the world," her mother said, starting to cry but stopping herself.

"Really, Mama? Do you mean it? Because I would love nothing more. Ichabod has promised me that we will do that, but I was so afraid of how it would make you and Papa feel," said Katrina.

"I want what makes you happiest, Katrina, and if this man makes you happy and he gives you the life he's promised, then I will celebrate your marriage with a happy heart when the day comes. I've seen you happier than I ever thought you could be, and if this man is the reason, then I can't in good conscience stand in the way. We will figure out what to do with the farm and estate when the time comes. But first let's focus on your wedding."

"Wedding? Who said we're getting married? Did Ichabod ask Papa for my hand?" Katrina felt as if her life was living her, and she felt herself being swept away.

"Yes, my dear. I assumed you knew he asked your father after dinner the other night. I'm sorry I've ruined his surprise. My goodness, I've been a poor mother these past several weeks, so consumed by the festival and the ball, when your courtship should have been my focus. But you're so smart, Katrina, so levelheaded. You've always known what you wanted since you were a little girl, so I've never had to worry about you; I always know you'll make the right choices. But that's no excuse. The moment your father told me Ichabod asked for your hand I should have come to you to see how you felt," she said, taking Katrina's hand.

"Don't be silly, Mama. I love you. You've always been a good mother, even more so lately." She kissed her mama on the cheek, careful not to disturb her beautiful makeup. "It means so much to me how supportive you've been, it's honestly really surprising."

"I want what makes you happiest, my sweet girl.

Shall we go down and join the party? I see your father didn't dress in costume, but he does look rather handsome, don't you think?" she said, smiling.

"He looks very handsome, Mama, and in a way he *is* in costume since he rarely dresses up," she said with a laugh.

As Katrina and Regina headed down the stairs, they saw Ichabod walk through the front door. Like her father and Brom, he wasn't in costume but had chosen to dress in a dandy suit. Ichabod usually looked quite dashing even if his clothes looked a little too large for him most of the time, but this evening he looked especially natty in various shades of green, even if he seemed a bit more nervous than usual.

"Don't be surprised if he asks you to marry him this evening, Katrina. Your father said that was his plan." She stepped back at Katrina's reaction. "You don't look pleased, though. I thought you'd be happy."

"I am pleased, I suppose. I just wish Ichabod had asked me first. I hate feeling like my entire life is being decided by men." Katrina tried to banish the overwhelming feeling of dread that was washing over her. Like her mother, she thought this moment would make her happy, but that familiar feeling of being ushered along by others was starting to make her feel trapped. She wished just for once she could direct her own life.

"I understand how you feel, my dear. I felt the same when my father and yours talked about our engagement before your father asked me to marry him, but that's how it's done. I don't think Ichabod was trying to go behind your back," said Regina. "Who knows, maybe he has something romantic planned for later this evening. One thing is certain, he does love you." She took Katrina's hand. "Now let's go downstairs and greet our guests, shall we?" she said, and kissed Katrina on the cheek.

Katrina thought perhaps her mother was right. Breaking up with Brom and this courtship with Ichabod were both her choice. She was going to live the life she always wanted with Ichabod, so she couldn't understand why she was feeling so ill at ease.

The party was in full swing by the time Katrina and Regina made their way downstairs. There was a band in the double parlor playing a lively tune. Happy couples of all ages were dancing the reel, while other guests chatted in clusters as they watched the dancers. There was live music in every wing of the house, and everywhere Katrina looked she saw happy faces. Her mother's party was a success.

Guests were milling around the room with plates of food piled high, and children were bobbing for apples on the front porch and playing tag in the mock cemetery. Katrina loved watching the little witches, ghosts, and skeletons running about, and wondered who would be here to continue these traditions if she and Ichabod were off traveling. Then something remarkable happened: Brom joined the children in the cemetery. He stretched out his arms like a great beast growling and roaring, and laughing when the children ran away from him screaming. This was the Brom Katrina missed, the man she had loved, and for the briefest of moments, she saw herself in the future with Brom, laughing at their children as they ran around the cemetery.

What will become of the farm and the estate and, more importantly, these fine people and our beloved town if I leave? she thought, looking at her neighbors, people she loved and grew up with filling her family's home with so much cheer. And she realized what was causing her so much trepidation. Her parents had spoken of her duty to the estate and to the people of Sleepy Hollow for so long it was like an abstract notion, but this evening she felt the weight of it, the reality, and she wasn't sure she had it in her to let everyone down. She felt like her heart was being pulled in two different directions.

"Good evening, my pirate queen." It was Ichabod, taking her hand and kissing it. She smiled until she noticed Brom was watching from a distance, causing the pangs of guilt to surge through her again. "What's troubling you, my sweet Katrina?" he asked, his eyes moving to Brom's direction as he returned to the party, leaving the children in the cemetery. "Has he been bothering you? Shall I talk to him?" he added.

"No, Ichabod, there is no need to kick the poor man while he's down."

"You no longer have feelings for him, then?" he said.

"No more than one would have for a childhood friend, or even a brother." But she wasn't sure if that was true. "I've never hidden my feelings for Brom from you. I was in love with him, but we became completely different people as we got older." She noticed Brom making his way over to them, and to her surprise, she felt nervous, wondering what Brom would think of her costume.

"Hello, Katrina, you look beautiful. Are you that

lady pirate you mentioned when we last had dinner here together?"

"Yes, I'm surprised you remembered," she said, making Brom laugh.

"I made it a point to read about her after that night and found there are a great many more female pirates than I expected. Anne Bonny, for example, now she's an interesting woman. Did you know she and Mary were on the same ship?"

"I didn't know you were such an avid reader, Brom," said Crane, "or that such things intrigued you." Crane didn't look convinced that Brom was being genuine, but Katrina didn't like this side of Crane, trying to catch him out like this.

"Well, I've had a lot more time on my hands after work lately," he said, tugging at Katrina's heart.

"Brom has always had a great love of good stories since we were young." It hadn't occurred to Katrina that Brom had less time for reading and the other things they enjoyed when he started working for her father, who had been training him to take over the farm when he and Katrina married, and Katrina suddenly felt selfish for holding that against him "You seem much changed to me, Brom, ever since the night . . ." She broke off because she didn't want to mention his encounter with the Headless Horseman. It was a sore subject for Brom, and she'd promised she wouldn't tell a soul. The last thing he'd want was her mentioning it in front of Ichabod. And she wondered if Brom's encounter with the Headless Horseman had taught him a lesson; he seemed humbler and certainly far less mean-spirited with Ichabod since it happened, so much more like the Brom she had once loved.

"I've had a lot of time to think about things," he said, then quickly changed the subject. "As usual, your mama outdid herself. Everything looks magnificent. Especially the decorations; the ones in the fields are so eerie. I was surprised to see she fashioned some to look like our most famous ghosts. One was peeking at me from behind an oak tree in the grove on my way in from the main gate, and I would swear she looked as if she was speaking to me!"

Katrina didn't know what he was talking about. They had only draped gossamer in the tree branches to resemble ghosts.

"That's strange, Mama didn't tell me she was planning something so elaborate. I wonder how she could have pulled off such a thing?" she said, looking out the window, trying to see if she could get a glimpse of what Brom was talking about.

"It is well known the dead walk the earth on All Hallows' Eve, or so the legends would have us believe," said Ichabod, finally finding a way to break into the conversation. "I would imagine such apparitions are even more prevalent in Sleepy Hollow, being such a haunted town. Did you know the tradition of dressing in costume on this night originated so the living may blend in with the dead?"

This seemed to really disturb Brom, who was now also looking out the window with trepidation. "Yes, Ichabod, we know." Katrina realized she was being a little short with him because she was feeling conflicted, and he was annoying her, and she decided she needed to clear her head for a moment.

"I'm going to see if my mama needs any help. Shall I bring you gentlemen some pumpkin tarts and hot chocolate with brandy when I return?"

"That would be lovely, my sweet Katrina," said Crane, making a point to touch her tenderly on the arm, but Brom didn't notice. He was still looking out the window. Katrina couldn't tell if Brom could actually see something out there in the trees, or if he was lost in his thoughts. She hated the idea of him still being tormented by the memories of that terrifying evening with the Headless Horseman, but she had a feeling it still haunted him.

"I think Brom could use a bit of extra brandy in his chocolate, my dearest. He seems a little spooked by the ghost he saw in the oak grove," Ichabod said with a rather smug look on his face. Katrina didn't like this side of Crane, but she understood where it was coming from. After all, Brom had teased him mercilessly in the past.

"Now, Ichabod, I'm sure if you were terrorized by the Headless Horseman on Sleepy Hollow Road you'd be spooked if you saw a ghost as well. Stop teasing him," she said with a slightly stern look for Crane. Then, realizing her mistake, she quickly added, "Shall we meet in the sitting room upon my return?" She felt terrible, even though she was sure Brom hadn't heard them, still distracted by something outside or lingering in his memory. "I shouldn't have said that, Ichabod. Please don't mention it to Brom," she said under her breath. "I'm counting on you to be a gentleman."

Katrina regretted her slip and her decision to leave them alone as she made her way around the party looking for her mother. It seemed everyone was still having a wonderful time, dancing and playing parlor games and singing along with the band.

As with most years, the older guests made their way home before it got too late, making an early night of it, except the Irvings. She laughed when she saw Mr. Irving in his wolf costume wearing a blindfold, spinning around in a circle and then groping at the air, surrounded by the other participants in the game, laughing. Even though the Van Tassels had provided carriages to ensure all their guests would make it safely home in the later hours, the eldest in the community felt more at ease tucked safely within their own homes before the clock tower chimed midnight, the Witching Hour, on All Hallows' Eve.

As she searched for her mother, happy to see everyone enjoying themselves, Katrina would never know for certain the exact conversation that transpired between Brom and Ichabod after she left them alone. Everyone in Sleepy Hollow seemed to have a different version of what happened. Katrina, of course, had her own theories, which were later confirmed after speaking with Brom. But it seemed after Katrina left them alone in the vestibule, Ichabod and Brom finally and awkwardly made their way to the sitting room, where Baltus sat in his favorite chair near the fireplace.

"Ah, Baltus! I see you've secured your favorite spot for the ghost stories. Is it that time already?" asked Brom, looking happy to see a friendly face. Baltus looked up and seemed disappointed to see Crane was standing there as well.

"Where is Katrina? Off helping her mother?" he asked.

"Indeed she is, sir," said Crane. "Though I suppose after tonight I will be calling you Papa." Crane took no pains hiding delight in letting it slip in front of Brom he was going to propose to Katrina that evening. The fire in the hearth was crackling, larger and more robust than usual so it could warm the room, which was open to the elements that evening. With the French doors open, they had an even more spectacular view of the oak grove, and the little ghosts and ghouls who were still playing tag in the cemetery. Brom could see some of the parents were collecting their children, under protest of course, because they too were eager to get home before the Witching Hour even though it was still a couple of hours away. Brom had always had the privilege of staying late on occasions like these, being part of the family, though he wasn't sure how he fit into the Van Tassels' lives now that he wasn't marrying Katrina.

"Now, Crane, there is no need to rub it in Brom's face," said Baltus.

"That's fine, Baltus," Brom said. "The better man won. It seems like Crane here will be able to give Katrina the life she truly wants." He walked over to the open French doors that looked out into the oak grove. He seemed to be wondering what ghostly presences lurked among the dark shadows.

Just then Regina popped her head into the sitting room. "Baltus, dear, Mr. Irving is being put into a carriage by his Mrs. Irving. She thinks he's had enough frivolity for the evening, but he refuses to leave until he has said his good-byes. I promise you may return to the comfort of your chair momentarily," she said, laughing. "And, gentlemen, Katrina will be back shortly with some refreshments. I'm sorry I've kept her busy for so long," she said before leaving Crane and Brom alone. The moment she did, Crane started in on Brom.

"Do you really think you're fooling anyone with all your talk of pirates and reading? You're even more of a fool than I thought you were," said Crane, coming up behind Brom with a taunting lilt to his voice.

Brom didn't turn around; he was still looking intently at something in the oak grove. Something had caught his eye.

"Be quiet for once in your life, Crane! Look, do you see that?" he said, squinting to get a better look.

"You can't trick me, Brom. I know you didn't really see the Headless Horseman that night, and you're not seeing anything now, you're just trying to frighten me off and make Katrina feel sorry for you, but it won't work."

Brom snapped his head around, grabbed Crane by the collar, and pulled him closer "Look! Right there!" he said, pointing to an exceptionally large black horse running down the center of the oak grove. Its coat was glistening in the candlelight, like it was covered in an oily black sheen. "It's the Headless Horseman!" he said, his hand shaking as it had when he told Katrina about his encounter.

"Take your hands off me, sir!" Crane said, scrambling backward away from Brom.

Within moments, a group of men were gathered at the perimeter of the grove, talking with each other, likely wondering where the horse had come from.

One of the men ran off toward the stable while the others stayed on the sidelines keeping an eye on the horse, and another man gathered up the children who were playing in the cemetery and ushered them inside.

"It looks like the situation is well in hand. It's likely just a horse that got out of the stables," said Crane, finally regaining his footing. "Brom, come away from the window and sit down. Your brooding is unseemly." Brom turned around to respond and was surprised to see Crane sitting in Baltus's chair near the fire.

"You'll want to get up before Baltus returns," he said, walking over and taking his usual place in the wooden rocking chair.

"Just trying it on for size," said Crane, leaning back with his hands behind his head, legs stretched out in his gangly fashion, looking smugger than Brom had ever seen him, which was quite a feat, since Crane seemed to make a point of being nothing but smug.

"From the sound it, I don't imagine you'll be spending much time close to your hearth, not with all the traveling you and Katrina have planned," said Brom, trying to calm his nerves, and using all of his will not to punch Crane straight in the face.

"You really are a dolt, aren't you? Do you really think I plan to travel the world when I have everything here I could possibly need?"

Brom shouldn't have been surprised by Crane's reply but found that he was. "I don't understand. You promised Katrina you would travel together."

Even Crane's laugh managed to sound smug and insulting. "Katrina is a young, foolish girl who doesn't know her own mind or what is best for her. Once we are married, she will take her rightful place by my side and we shall serve as pillars of the community." Crane was now smiling, oozing with conceit and pride.

Brom had spent the past several weeks regretting his treatment of Katrina—playing their conversations over in his mind, flinching at his own words—and his heart broke because he knew there was nothing he could do to win back the woman he loved. But hearing Crane speak this way, he truly understood now why Katrina had become so disenchanted with him. Hearing his own words coming from such a smug little turd like Crane made him realize how he had sounded to Katrina. Disgusted with Crane and himself, he got up from his seat at the fireplace and went back to the window to see if the men had caught the horse. Crane didn't deserve her after all, and he was going to do everything he could to make sure she didn't marry him.

"I wish I had done things differently with Katrina. I stopped listening to what she truly wanted. If she would give me another chance, I would give her the life she wanted; that's how much I love her," he said, looking out the window at the men searching the oak grove with torches, the horse nowhere in sight. He could hear Crane laughing at him from Baltus's chair and it sent bolts of anger and regret though his body. "If Katrina takes me back, I will leave Sleepy Hollow if that's what she wants. I would willfully and happily give up the farm and all the money that comes with it if I could just have her back again, and I would spend the rest of my days doing whatever I could to make her happy," said Brom.

"Don't be a fool. Katrina will never love you again, not like that. There is nothing you can do to win her back," said Crane, laughing harder, with the snide look on his face.

"This isn't about winning her back, Crane. This is about protecting her from you!"

"Protect her from me? What do you have to offer her, Brom? Do you really think she would want to be with you, when she has me? You don't deserve her, a man who was too stupid to see a good thing you had while you had it," said Crane, laughing even louder.

But Brom wasn't listening. He was distracted by what was going on in the oak grove. As the men were walking away, having given up on finding the horse, he saw the black stallion appear again—and it was galloping toward them. But this time a black figure was astride the horse with a long sword raised in the air.

"Great Hollow's Ghost, watch out!" Brom yelled out the open French doors, but before the men turned around, the horse and rider vanished. "Good heavens! Did you see that, Crane? It was the Headless Horseman!" Brom's hands were shaking, and terror ripped through his entire body, making him want to flee.

"Oh, stop it, Brom; you're grasping and making yourself look even more foolish than usual," Crane said with a sneer.

"No, really, man. I saw him." He walked over to Crane and stood in front of him, his back to the fire. "I know what you think of me, but I'm not a liar. And I know I was a fool not to see what a wonderful woman I had in Katrina, but I haven't lost my mind; I know what I saw!" he said, trying to urge Crane to come with him back to the window.

"I won't fall for your trickery, Brom. I know what you're up to. You're trying to frighten me in order to win back Katrina's heart, but it won't work. You lost your chance with her, Brom. You've lost everything."

"I will always regret losing Katrina's affections; the ghost of our love will haunt me until the last of my days," said Brom, trying to hold back his tears. "But it is a more sinister ghost I'm concerned about in this moment."

"You lost something far more precious than Katrina's love. You lost everything that comes along with it, the farm, the estate, and her *money*," said Crane with a malicious look on his face. "Did it occur to you that all you had to do was pretend you love the same things she does, encourage her ridiculous dreams of becoming an author, pretend you wanted to travel the world, and once you were married steer her in the direction you wanted?" he said, with a look so vicious it contorted his face in a manner that showed Brom who Crane really was.

"You're vile, Crane. Reprehensible and cruel, and I will do everything in my power to make sure Katrina never marries you," said Brom, now towering over Crane, who was still sitting in Baltus's chair. "Stand up, Crane," said Brom, grabbing him by the collar. "I think it's time we have a talk with Baltus and tell him what you've been up to." He dragged Crane to his feet, Crane's arms and legs flailing like a scarecrow in the wind.

"Take your hands off me, you fool!" said Crane, taking an awkward swing at Brom and missing.

"I'm not going to fight you, though goodness knows you deserve it." Brom backed away, but Crane put up his fists, his head lurching from one side to the other and swinging his fists wildly, landing a lucky blow square in Brom's face. The men heard a sickening crack that could only be the breaking of his nose, and then the blood came pouring down Brom's face. By the time Brom returned the blow and knocked Ichabod to the floor, a group of people had come upon them to see what the commotion was about.

"Do you see what this brute has done to me? Jealous of my relationship with Katrina, he punched me unprovoked. He's a beast and should be put down," said Crane, wiping the blood from his mouth with a contemptuous smile as Baltus and the other men dragged Brom into the hall, where Katrina was standing, shocked at what she had just seen.

TWENTY

THE DIARY OF KATRINA VAN TASSEL

BEWARE OF THE HEADLESS HORSEMAN

I stood, frozen, as I watched my father breaking up the fight between Brom and Ichabod, the mugs and dessert plates broken at my feet. I was heartbroken, and sickened by what I just saw, and I wondered if Ichabod knew I had heard every insidious word he had just spoken to Brom.

⌣

Katrina ran up to her room in a rage, ripping off her hat and belt—the costume she was so proud of—and throwing them across the room. She paced back and forth, trying to figure out what to do next. She was enraged. She flung open her balcony doors and stepped out to see that the party was breaking up now, and the last of the younger guests were going home. No doubt Brom and Ichabod's display had soured the celebratory mood.

She stood there on the balcony, watching everyone take their leave, saying their good-byes, and getting into carriages. Then Brom came angrily stomping out the front door, yelling at Crane. Katrina moved behind one of the bat decorations so they wouldn't see her as she looked down on them.

"Mark my words, Crane, you will never marry Katrina!" She had never seen Brom so angry. Her father came out and said something to him she couldn't quite make out, but it soon became clear. "I'm too angry, Baltus. We'll talk tomorrow! And no, I don't need a bloody carriage!" he yelled, storming off into the darkness.

After a moment, Crane came out, followed by Katrina's mother.

"But I don't understand. What happened?" asked Regina.

"He said some very offensive things about our Katrina," said Crane, fussing over his suit, which had gotten rumpled during the fisticuffs with Brom.

"That doesn't sound like Brom," said Baltus, eyeing Crane.

"I assure you, good sir, that's exactly what happened. I think he is smarting because Katrina has chosen me over him. I just wish his brutish behavior hadn't thwarted my plans to propose to Katrina this evening," said Crane.

"Not to worry, dear. I am sure there will be another opportunity," Regina said, but Kat could see both of her parents didn't look convinced Ichabod was telling them the whole story. "I'm sorry Katrina isn't here to say good-bye, but she was very upset by what happened between you and Brom. I will go upstairs and talk with her. I'm sure everything will work out just fine."

"Did she hear what we . . . what Brom said?" asked Crane.

"I don't think so," said Baltus, still eyeing Crane warily. "I think she came in when I was breaking up your fight, but of course I can't be sure."

Regina put her hand on Crane's shoulder. "All right, my dear, let me get you a carriage," she said, looking to see if there was one available.

"I think all the carriages are in use, Regina," said

Baltus. "Besides, I do believe Mr. Crow came here by horse, did he not? And a brave young man like Ichabod here doesn't need a carriage now, does he?" Baltus smiled at Crane like a cat eyeing a canary. It gave Katrina a small sense of satisfaction. She could tell her dad was onto Crane and was enjoying toying with him.

"Indeed . . . I . . . do not," he stammered, looking up at Katrina's balcony. She was sure he had seen her, but she moved farther into the shadows so she would be out of sight.

"I shall fetch your horse myself. It's the plowing horse, is it not?" said Baltus, laughing to himself on the way to the stable.

Katrina watched as her father walked away and her mother said her good-byes. "Good night, then, Ichabod," said Regina. "If you'll excuse me, I should see if there are any lingering guests who need to be roused and sent off to their beds." She returned inside, leaving Crane alone in the foreboding darkness.

"Here you go, Crane. Have a nice ride home," said Baltus with a wry smile, handing the horse's reins over to the gangly fellow.

Before mounting his horse, Kat could see Crane felt like someone was watching him. It was a tingling sensation that something wasn't quite right, and then he saw her. Katrina was now standing in full view on her balcony silently looking down on him. They locked eyes, but something caught her eye in the distance. Crane turned around quickly to see what she was looking at so intensely but saw nothing there. And when he turned around, the look on Katrina's face horrified him.

"Beware of the Headless Horseman," she said, then turned around and went back into her bedroom.

TWENTY-ONE

THE DIARY OF KATRINA VAN TASSEL

THE MISADVENTURES OF ICHABOD CRANE

It was the very Witching Hour of night as Ichabod perused his travel home. The sky grew darker and darker as one by one the stars blinked out their lights. The writhing clouds obscured the moon from sight and never had the schoolmaster felt so melancholy, so utterly alone, and the nearer he approached the hollow the more dismal he became.

꒐

C rane had made a dreadful mistake. He should have never bragged to Brom as he did, and he was deeply afraid Katrina had heard what he said. He couldn't be certain of course, but by the look on Katrina's face, he was almost sure she had. And if by some chance Katrina did not hear his conversation with Brom, he was sure she would hear about it by morning, and so would Baltus.

Beware of the Headless Horseman. Never had words sent more terror surging through him; it shook his entire body and chilled his core.

Astride his plow horse and whistling to himself to calm his nerves, Crane traversed Sleepy Hollow Road under a menacing canopy of trees that seemed more like gnarled witches' hands than branches. He cursed himself as his horse slowly made its way, not sure what he was more afraid of: the Headless Horseman, or losing Katrina's hand in marriage and the extravagant life he'd envisioned for himself that came along with it.

The moon peeked through the skeletal branches, only to be enveloped by clouds that looked like menacing hands, choking all the light from the sky and leaving him in darkness. A gust of wind caused the autumn leaves to swirl around him while an owl screeched in the distance, followed closely by the howl of a wolf. Suddenly, he saw a wailing ghost dancing on the wind that turned his blood cold, only to find it was just his fevered imagination when the clouds shifted and the moonlight revealed the terrifying ghost was only a hollowed-out tree.

And even though he was jumping at every shadow and feared he would see the Headless Horseman at each turn of the path, the most haunting image from that night was Katrina's wrathful gaze peering down at him from her balcony. All of his plans were in ruin now, and he wondered what tomorrow would bring if he indeed survived this night. He speculated if Brom had indeed met the Headless Horseman on this dreaded path or if he was simply trying to spook him into leaving town, but he couldn't vanquish the fear of the headless Hessian as he crossed a small bridge over a pond. From the black water, croaking toads seemed to say his name, singing in concert with the wind on the reeds, filling the very atmosphere with dread. It seemed to Ichabod all the Witching Hour creatures had come out to sing his funeral dirge, including a murder of crows who took their screeching song to the sky, revealing his location to the demon Hessian.

Then he heard it, the sound of a galloping horse approaching, causing his heart to race, only to find it was the sound of pussy willows thumping violently in the wind on a hollowed-out oak. He stood there laughing at himself for being so afraid, and then his laugh was matched by a sinister and otherworldly laugh, mocking him.

It was the Headless Horseman!

He was right there in front of him on the path, lurid and frightening, sending panic though his entire body. Ichabod shuddered as he locked eyes with the demon horse, which was rearing up as the Headless Horseman raised his sword overhead, his cape blowing on a supernatural wind as he charged at Ichabod.

Ichabod urged his horse forward as best he could, and the Headless Horseman pursued them through the woods. The demon horse's breath was hot on his neck, and he could feel the horseman slice through the air again and again, his sword missing Ichabod's neck by mere inches, causing his blood to run cold. He could feel the swish of the blade like a violent wind. So full of terror was he that Ichabod didn't notice he was hurtling toward the sharp drop of a cliff until he and his horse were careening down a ravine and into a creek. He smashed into a tree and sat, dazed and blinking, in the dark water. Then an image rose up above him; the Headless Horseman had circled around and cut him off at the path.

Crane was sure in that moment he would die. Then, behind the ghostly rider he saw the covered bridge ahead in the distance. Brom's words echoed in his mind, *Only when you've reached the other side of the covered bridge will you be safe.* He kicked his heels into his poor horse, coaxing it to run as fast as it could. He kicked it again and again, as they bolted across the bridge, not daring to look back until they finally made it to the other side. His horse threw him off, leaving him dazed as it ran off into the woods, leaving Crane alone on the path, breathless and woozy. When he looked up, still dizzy from his fall, he saw the Headless Horseman on the other side of the bridge, watching him. He had a strange feeling. It reminded him of the way Katrina had looked at him from the balcony. The last thing he saw was a flaming jack-o'-lantern hurtling in his direction.

On the following morning, the only thing left on the scene was a smashed pumpkin and Ichabod's hat.

Ichabod Crane was never seen in Sleepy Hollow again.

TWENTY-TWO

A TRUE KATRINA

Kat and Isadora were in the library snuggled in the reading window nook and realized they had lost track of time reading Katrina's diary, when they looked up and saw it was completely dark outside. Kat looked down at her phone, which was sitting on a table her mom had set up with sandwiches and coffee for her and Isadora that were still there untouched. "What is it? What's wrong?" asked Isadora.

"I missed my final. I was supposed to make it up today and completely flaked on it." She slammed her phone back down and felt disappointed in herself.

"I'm sure Headmaster Toad will let you make it up, especially with everything going on."

Isadora was probably right, but it wasn't like Kat to

forget something so important. "I hope so," Kat said, looking off.

"What else is bothering you? Did Blake or one of his friends send a text or something?"

"It's just . . . how did Katrina know what happened, if Crane just vanished? Who told her what happened to him that night? It feels like there is more to this story," said Kat.

"I don't know, I guess the Headless Horseman told her?" Isadora wondered. "There are parts of the diary where Katrina writes about things other people told her."

Kat felt like they were missing something; it seemed strange the diary would just end there. "Maybe my mom knows where Katrina's other diaries are. I want to know if the Horseman told her he was the one who chased Ichabod away. And I want to know what happened to him."

"Well, I know what happened to him. He ended up in a town nearby, got married, and had a ton of kids. Family legend says he always swore it was the Headless Horseman who chased him through the hollow. What's strange, though, is he wasn't buried there. We don't know where Uncle Ichabod's grave is."

Suddenly the room seemed to shift, as if everything went out of focus for just the briefest of moments. Kat and Isadora felt it like a lurching in their stomachs, like being dropped too fast in an elevator.

"The Horseman didn't frighten Ichabod away," said a voice. *"I did."*

Both girls turned at the voice, trying to take in what was happening.

There, standing before them, was Katrina, vivid as life. She was a small, curvy woman with long blond hair pulled up into a bun, her big, bright eyes sparkling at them as she smiled. She was exactly as Kat imagined her. But she hadn't simply imagined her, had she? She remembered her. This was the woman from her childhood, the woman she had been seeing the past few days. Kat thought she looked as though she had stepped off the pages of a fairy tale, and then she laughed, realizing she had, except it wasn't a fairy story, it was a ghost story.

"Katrina? It was *you* all along?" said Kat, getting up from the nook.

"Indeed, my sweet girl," said the ghostly woman. *"I'm so sorry I frightened you these past few days. I was only trying to protect you, but Blake had other ideas."*

Kat was in shock because she was actually talking

to Katrina, and she was trying take it all in. She had so many questions.

"What do you mean you scared Ichabod away?"

"It was no ghostly specter. It was me."

"So, the Headless Horseman isn't real? Did you scare Brom as well?" Isadora asked, joining Kat and Katrina.

"The Headless Horseman is real. He is the one who went after Brom, but it was I who chased Ichabod out of Sleepy Hollow. I was so angry after hearing everything Ichabod said that night, the next thing I knew I was grabbing a cloak and throwing it over the remainder of my costume. I grabbed one of the jack-o'-lanterns and got on my father's horse. I don't think I even thought about what I was doing, I just wanted to make Crane pay for what he did to me."

"Well, it was brilliant! All these years almost everyone thought it was really the Headless Horseman, and all along it was you," said Isadora.

Both of the girls were in shock. They couldn't believe Katrina was really there after reading about her for so long.

"Thank you, Isadora Crane. I have much to say to you," said Katrina, drifting off to another place, causing the room to shift again, as if for a moment they were in another place. *"But first I must take a proper look at my*

namesake." She moved closer to Kat and smiled at her. *"Look at you, my little Katrina. So strong and brave. So smart and independent. I am happy you're finally free from your fear and doubt."*

"But I have so many lingering doubts. I want so much to live up to your legacy, but I also want to live a life that is mine. I am so afraid of disappointing you."

"And you're afraid of ending up like me. I see into your heart, and I've listened to your fears by the Oldest Tree. They sounded so much like my own. But please know, I am here because I want to be, because I chose to be here with Brom. The moment I heard Brom tell Ichabod he would be willing to leave Sleepy Hollow behind and travel the world with me I knew I wanted nothing more than to stay here with him, because in that moment I had what I always wanted, a choice. And I knew in my heart if Brom and I had left, Sleepy Hollow wouldn't be what it is today. It would be an empty place, left only with its ghosts and no one to share their stories," she said, looking as if she became lost in her thoughts again, as if she was in two places at once, drifting between them.

"Then don't I have a responsibility to stay?" asked Kat, feeling that old panic that she would be stuck in Sleepy Hollow forever.

"You won't be stuck here forever, my darling. I want you

to go to college, to live the life you've always wanted, and who knows, maybe your new path will lead you back here and you will come visit me by the Oldest Tree and tell me of your adventures. But know no matter what you do, I will be proud of you, because you are a true Katrina." Kat was struck by her words, *a true Katrina.* She felt them deeply within her heart and wanted nothing more than to hug Katrina, but she drifted off again, as if she were in another place, phasing in and out of view.

"*You're so much like Ichabod, Isadora,*" said Katrina, finally drifting back to them again, her face serene and her eyes flashing with sadness.

"I'm nothing like my uncle Ichabod." Isadora clutched Kat's hand, and Kat squeezed it trying to give her courage. "I promise you, I promise you both, there is nothing of Ichabod within me."

"*You mistake me, my dear, I see the virtues in him I loved and cherished most inside of you, it's no wonder my namesake is so fond of you. I can see into your heart, Isadora Crane, and I know you will not hurt Kat, or else you wouldn't be standing here now.*" And Kat knew what she meant—if Isadora had intended to hurt her, Katrina and the Headless Horseman would have run her out of town. It was both a comforting and frightening thought.

"I'm so sorry I wasn't always there to protect you, Kat. Blake was cunning, he found ways to keep me from you, but I promise I won't ever let that happen again. There is so much I want to tell you, so much you need to know, but I am running out of time. Blake has done something horrible, something I'm not sure can be undone. You saw the evidence of it in the hollow, the old headstone that wasn't marked. He did it after you broke up with him, Kat. He was desperate, he blamed me and wanted me to suffer, but he went too far and has let something foul into his heart. Promise me, if the worst happens, you will find my other diaries. There is more to this story." Just then Katrina started to scream. It was the most terrifying sound, she was screaming so loudly it was rattling the windows, and it made both of them cover their ears in pain. The room shifted more violently this time; ghost-like flashes of the oak grove were moving in and out of focus, making Kat feel as if she were in her library and in the grove at once.

"What's happening? What's wrong?" Kat didn't know how to help Katrina. She couldn't stand seeing her in such pain. Katrina fell to the floor, releasing a sob with each wave of pain that came over her, making her body convulse violently, sending shock waves through the room, causing it to shake violently.

"What's happening? Who is doing this to you?" asked Isadora. Both of the girls were leaning over her, trying to figure out how to help.

"It's Blake!" she said, writhing on the floor as deep gashes appeared on her body. Kat and Isadora jumped back, horrified. Deep gruesome wounds were appearing across her arms, legs, and face.

"What do you mean, it's Blake? How is he doing this?" Kat and Isadora trembled in fear and helplessness as Katrina writhed in pain.

"He's trapped me and the Headless Horseman inside the Oldest Tree!"

"But I don't understand—you're here!" said Kat.

"I am in all places. I am with the Oldest Tree and with you. I am part of Sleepy Hollow as it is part of me."

Katrina suddenly became rigid; she howled as her body stretched out, reaching the lofted ceilings, her arms growing into twisted oak branches, her legs turning into the hollowed-out trunk. The roots of the trunk crashed through the floor, and her branches penetrated the walls, bookshelves, and ceiling, and smashed through windows. More ghastly gashes appeared in violent succession, each time with a burst of blood. Katrina's screams pierced their ears, and before they even realized what was happening, they were no longer in Kat's library, they were in the hollow not far from the Oldest Tree.

"How did we get here? What happened?" Both girls looked around, confused, and felt like they might faint. They were disoriented and unsteady on their feet, and sickened by what happened to Katrina.

"I'm afraid I brought you here with me, my girls. I didn't intend to, but it took everything within me. I don't have the strength to escape the oak; please help us else Blake banish our spirits into the darkness and I will never see you again."

Katrina's voice was like a whisper on the wind, but they knew she was trapped inside the oak with the Headless Horseman. They were at Blake's mercy.

They could see Blake hacking away at the tree. With each strike of the axe, they heard the guttural screams of Katrina and the Headless Horseman coming from within the venerable oak, blood spraying so violently it sent Blake careening backward. He was in such a state of madness every time the blood sent him flying, he would get right back up and charge the tree again.

"How do we help them? I don't know what to do." Kat looked to Isadora, hoping she would have the answer.

"I don't, either. He's completely out of his mind. How are we supposed to stop him?" They heard him screaming in the distance, yelling at Katrina as he struck another blow to the tree.

"This is your fault, poisoning Kat against me! Everything was fine until she started reading your diary!" He hacked away at the tree over and over, this time not affected by the blood gushing out at him.

The girls watched in terror as Blake reeled in a state of frenzy and delirium. They wanted to do something to help but were afraid of being caught up in his mania—he was like a man possessed. The girls watched in horror as Blake's face and body contorted, his expression moving from rage to fear.

"Do you think I'm a fool, Katrina? Of course I knew it was you who chased me out of Sleepy Hollow!"

"Something isn't right. Blake is a gaslighting douche but he isn't a psychopath." Isadora's face transformed, a look of pure terror seized her. "Do you think he is possessed? He's acting like he's two different people."

"Possessed? By who?" Kat asked, but then it hit her. "Oh my god, Ichabod! Katrina said it had to do with the headstone we found; could that be Ichabod's grave?"

"What are we supposed to do? He has an *axe*." Kat could see Isadora was horrified, frozen in fear.

"We have to do something," said Kat, but Isadora was transfixed watching Blake.

"That's my uncle? He's making him do that? Was Blake possessed by Ichabod the entire time? Was he getting some sort of revenge on you because you're Katrina's namesake?"

"No, Isadora, Blake was manipulative and corrupt before Ichabod invaded him. Blake chose his own path and paid the price by raising the spirit of your uncle to achieve his goal. Will you help Katrina defeat him, defeat them both? Will you stand with her against your own blood to save us?"

"Of course I will! What do we do?" Isadora grabbed Kat's hand. "How do we stop them?"

"Hold tight to Kat's hand, and give her strength as she says the words."

"What words?" Kat asked. "Do you know the words? You know more about this stuff than I do. What am I supposed to say?" Kat looked to Isadora, hoping she had the answer. She didn't know what to say, and she didn't know if she had the power to stop them. "You have to help me," Kat said, feeling desperate.

Isadora took Kat's hand, looked into her eyes, and said, "You know the words, Kat, they're inside of you."

"Say the words, Kat! Be brave. Save us," said Katrina, her voice so loud it filled the forest and caused the leaves to shower down upon them as the trees grew larger around them, their branches stretching to join each other, covering the hollow in darkness.

"What words? What do I say?" Kat screamed into the darkness, afraid Blake would hear her, but she was desperate as she watched Blake hack away at the tree, watching the blood spurt forth while screaming deviant madness as all the oak trees in the hollow grew to cyclopean heights, their roots bursting from the earth, causing the ground to quake and branches to crash into each other. The girls screamed. Kat glanced toward Isadora. "I need you. I don't know what to say."

Isadora squeezed Kat's hand. "I'm right here, Kat, but you don't need me. You can do this."

It was then Blake noticed them. Kat could feel his eyes lock on hers. He raised his axe and ran toward them. He looked monstrous, covered in blood, as he ran toward them.

Kat thought she had freed herself from him, but she saw she had to face another fear before she could truly be free of this monster, so she said the words:

"I call upon the ghosts of Sleepy Hollow in the name of

Katrina Van Tassel, to release her spirit, and take vengeance upon those who would do us harm!"

The forest was instantly filled with ghosts, all manner of them, old and young, some with faces Kat remembered and those who had died long before she or the first Katrina had been born. They swarmed the forest like a blighting plague, leaving thick black soot in their path as they surrounded the Oldest Tree, removing the salt that surrounded it, and then spreading its blight throughout the entire forest and into the town of Sleepy Hollow, enveloping it in darkness and despair. It was a terrifying sight, seeing the blackness envelop everything. The only light was that of the spirits shining through the darkness like stars peeking through a dark curtain of night. But nothing was so terrifying as the Headless Horseman and Katrina Van Tassel astride the spectral beast, bursting forth from the hollow of the tree, at last free from the wretched curse that had ensnared them both. The rider snatched Blake with one strong arm and galloped off into the darkness out of sight, taking Blake out of Kat's life forever.

Blake was never seen in Sleepy Hollow again.

EPILOGUE

THE ADVENTURES OF
KAT VAN TASSEL

I t's been many years since that terrifying night, and to this day the first Katrina and the Headless Horseman won't tell me what befell Blake or Ichabod Crane's spirit that evening.

"They won't be bothering you or Isadora ever again." That is all the Headless Horseman would say on the subject of Blake when he returned to the Oldest Tree, where he left Isadora and me standing on that horrifying night. Of course I wanted to know the truth, I wanted to know what became of him, but I left it alone. At least for a while.

"Thank you for saving us," I said, feeling oddly connected to this man. A dead man without a head. It was a connection that would not only endure but strengthen throughout my entire life. But that is another story.

"You saved us, Kat Van Tassel, by calling forth the spirits of this place, and by facing your fears. Thank you for awakening me, as Katrina did so many years ago."

"What do you mean? How did I wake you?"

"You sat by my tree writing about your dreams and desires, your wish for a different life, and you cried when your heart was broken, just as Katrina did before you. How could I not awaken? I wanted to protect you, as I tried to protect Katrina. It was my plan to run Ichabod out of Sleepy Hollow that night, frighten him as I did Brom, but when I saw Katrina on that horse, dressed as me, saw how strong and brave she was, I knew she didn't need my help, and I fell in love with her on that night and swore I would protect all who shared her name."

"Did Katrina know you were real? Did you ever show yourself to her?"

"When I knew she was safe, my spirit went back into the oak, but she knew I was real. My dear Katrina came to me every day and spoke to me at our tree; she told me of her life, the stories she had written, and how happy Brom made her. You're a brave woman, Kat, just like Katrina. I know she is proud of you, and when she is strong enough, she will come to you and tell you so herself and perhaps she will share the rest of her story with you. But for now, she and the other ghosts

of this place are at work restoring Sleepy Hollow by removing the blight caused by their pursuit of Blake and the spirit of Ichabod Crane. And now I must go to help them."

I could feel Isadora's hand trembling in mine as the Horseman spoke, and I squeezed it, trying to calm her.

"Don't be afraid, Isadora Crane. As I said, you have nothing to fear from me."

As he mounted his horse, a supernatural wind blew through the hollow, causing the autumn leaves to swirl around him as his horse reared up against the orange autumn sky. And without another word or warning, the Headless Horseman bolted down Sleepy Hollow Road, the wind trailing behind him, sweeping away the remainder of the blight that was left in the wake of the ghostly swarm.

As Isadora and I walked through the hollow, trailing far behind him, we saw that Sleepy Hollow was as the Horseman had described, restored. And waiting for us in the oak grove were my parents, who took both of us in their arms and hugged us again and again, relieved we were unharmed.

"Thank Sleepy Hollow's Ghost, you're safe. We were coming to find you," said my mom as my dad inspected us for injuries between his giant bear hugs.

"We're fine, Dad. You're hugging us too tightly," I said, making everyone laugh.

After that night, after we were back home again and we told my parents what happened, life was different in our house and very different in Sleepy Hollow. At least for a time.

It was quite a while before we saw Katrina and the Headless Horseman again, or any of Sleepy Hollow's ghosts for that matter. But they did come back. They were, as the Horseman said, resting after their exhausting adventure.

As for me and Isadora, our story was just beginning. As the ghosts returned, they revealed new mysteries and secrets to uncover, as we prepared for graduation from what would eventually become Katrina Van Tassel High. Just as we were bracing ourselves for new adventures away from Sleepy Hollow, it seemed there was more to the Legend of Sleepy Hollow than we could possibly fathom, but that is a story for another time.

THE END

ACKNOWLEDGMENTS

I probably wouldn't have written this book if it weren't for Anne Rice. She gave me the courage and inspiration to become a writer—to not be afraid of doing it wrong, breaking the rules, or creating a unique voice that was entirely my own. She showed me how powerful it could be to process my grief through writing, without which I am not sure I would have survived the loss of my sister.

Anne's accessibility, kindness, and graciousness to her readers was an inspiration, and my guide with my own lovely and amazing readers.

And she was an outspoken ally for the LGBTQ+ community, which meant the world to me as a young bi woman reading her books for the first time. It filled my heart with joy that someone I admired so greatly was not only a brilliant author, but a beautiful person as well.

She will be deeply missed.